PROJECT

LOGOS

ORION KEETS

ISBN
Paperback: 979-8-90321-005-3
Hardback: 979-8-90321-006-0

Dedication

For my mother and my sister

my first believers.

And for the line cooks I've worked with,

and the line cooks everywhere,

standing shoulder to shoulder in heat and chaos,

feeding people while quietly fighting their own wars.

This book comes from that fire.

Prologue:
The Desert Accord

Holloman Air Force Base: New Mexico – February 1954

The desert air was dry and bitter, but Eisenhower still felt the sweat trickle down the back of his neck. The hangar smelled of oil and ozone like a thunderstorm had passed through and forgotten to leave.

Five men stood in silence behind him: two generals, a physicist, a priest, and an aide who couldn't stop tapping his foot. They all stared at the same impossible thing.

The craft didn't sit on landing gear. It floated weightless, perfect, a silver teardrop defying the laws of man and God alike.

And then the door opened.

They were smaller than the President expected thin, almost fragile. Their black eyes reflected everything and revealed nothing. One moved forward without sound. Its voice didn't come from its mouth. It boomed in Eisenhower's skull like a thought that wasn't his own.

"Do not fear. We have watched over your kind since the first spark of your civilization."

Eisenhower swallowed. "If that's true, you've got a strange way of showing it. Where were you during the wars?"

The being tilted its head. "Wars are necessary. They shape destiny. But the time has come to end them."

A second figure glided forward, carrying something like a sphere of liquid light. It pulsed in rhythm with Eisenhower's heartbeat.

"A gift," the voice said. "Power without limit. Energy to light every city in your world. Medicine to end suffering. Peace for your species. All we ask in return is an accord."

Eisenhower's jaw tightened. "What kind of accord?"

"A partnership. We will guide you as we always have. We will protect you from the Others."

"The others?" the priest whispered, clutching his crucifix.

The being's eyes flickered. For the first time, Eisenhower thought he saw something hate, or maybe fear.

"They are not like us. They believe in chaos… in freedom. They interfered before, on your sister world. It cost them everything."

"Mars," the physicist muttered.

The lead being stepped closer so near Eisenhower could feel the chill coming off its skin.

"Sign the covenant, and we will ensure your survival. Refuse… and they will come. And when they do, your kind will perish as theirs did."

The President stared into those bottomless eyes and for the first time in his life he felt small. He thought of his oath, of the nation, of mankind. He thought of God and wondered if God was even listening.

Finally, he spoke. "You talk like you've been playing God for a long time."

The being's lips curved in something that might have been a smile or a warning.

"No, Mr. President. We are God."

The words echoed in his mind long after the sound was gone.

In the corner of the hangar, the priest whispered a single line of scripture, barely audible over the hum of the alien craft:

"And no marvel, for Satan himself is transformed into an angel of light."

Table of Contents

Chapter One:
Heat

The ticket machine screamed like it was mocking him. Orders spat out in a never-ending paper stream, curling on the stainless steel like some cosmic joke. Elias slammed a pan down, oil hissing like it had a grudge, and for a second, he thought about how good a cigarette would taste right now. Just one tray just enough to take the edge off the hum in his skull.

"Pick up! Fire two rib-eyes, mid-rare, on the fly!" The chef's voice cut through the heat, sharp as the knives stacked by the sink.

Elias muttered something under his breath, too low for anyone to catch, and dropped the steaks like he was punishing them for existing. His thin apron clung to him like a damp rag. Sweat ran down his spine, and his mind kept turning back to the car outside, where a pack of smokes waited like a promise. But he couldn't leave. Not now. Not with the clock ticking, the burners roaring, and the ghosts in his head whispering that he didn't belong there.

"Elias, where the hell's my scallops?"

He blinked for a second. He didn't know where he was. The kitchen snapped back into focus: steel, fire, voices. He looked down scallops still raw, sitting in the pan like pale little secrets.

"Coming, Chef!" he barked, too loud, and his hands moved on instinct. But something inside him didn't move. It stayed stuck, right there in the heat, wondering if this was all life had left for him.

And then, as he flipped the scallops, the hiss rising like a scream he smelled smoke. Not from the pan. From somewhere else.

It threaded through the heat like a ghost, thin and sharp, curling into his nose the way a cigarette would. For a second, he froze, spatula hanging in the air, eyes scanning the line. Nothing burning. Nothing on fire. Just the same chaos steam clouding, fryer spit, the chef barking.

But the smell stayed.

His mouth watered. God, he could almost feel the paper between his fingers, the first crackle of tobacco catching flame, the first pull filling his lungs. That slow, poisonous calm. He hadn't smoked since the shift started, but it was all he could think about now. Every nerve in his body tugged toward the back door, toward the alley toward escape.

"Elias!" The chef's voice slammed him back. "Move those scallops, or I'll move you!"

He snapped out of it, plating fast, hands moving like they belonged to someone else scallops, butter frizzle, microgreens like confetti. Beautiful, perfect, pointless.

The ticket rail spat again another order, screaming for attention. The printer whirred like a wasp in his ear. He hated that sound. Hated what it meant: that no matter how fast he moved, the line never ended. It wasn't cooking anymore; it was drowning. And the water was boiling.

The smoke came back, stronger this time. He caught it between orders sharp and sacred cutting through the smell of garlic and seared meat.

He lifted his head. Nothing. No flames. No black streak curling off a pan. No one else seemed to notice.

He wiped his forehead with the back of his wrist, sweat streaking the salt on his skin. His chest was tight. Maybe it wasn't smoke. Maybe it was just his brain cooking in the heat, his nerves fried like the baskets dropping behind him.

He thought about asking someone then didn't. Better to keep quiet. Better to keep moving.

By the time the rush broke by the time the last ticket dropped and the grill hissed like a tired animal the smell was gone. Just like that. Like it had never been there.

Elias stood at the line, staring at nothing. The noises faded the clang and the bark and the curses draining out of the kitchen until all he could hear was his own breath.

He pulled off his apron and felt how heavy it was, how wet. It hit the hook with a slap.

He walked out the back door without a word.

The night hit him in the face. Cool, black, wide open. He sucked in the air like it was water, like he'd been under too long.

The alley was empty except for the dumpster and the hum of the city beyond. He fished a cigarette from the crumpled pack in his pocket, hands shaking just enough to notice. The lighter clicked, flame flared. Smoke filled him.

Not the same smoke. Not the one from before this was his. This was real.

He closed his eyes on the first drag, letting it burn slow. And for a moment, he didn't feel like drowning.

But when he opened his eyes, something strange caught him: the faintest curl of gray slipping out from the cracks of the kitchen door behind him.

Just for a second.

Then it was gone.

Chapter Two:
Whispers In The Steam

The alley behind the restaurant smelled like rain and garbage, but to Elias, it smelled like freedom. Cigarette smoke curled around his face as he leaned against the slick brick wall, the burn in his lungs slowing his pulse for the first time in hours.

The night was warm, the air humming with the low growl of dumpsters and distant traffic. Somewhere, a train moaned across the city. BK came out of the back door with his usual swagger, apron still on, black hair matted with sweat. He held a cigarette between two fingers like a preacher with a Bible.

"Hey, man," BK said, exhaling a cloud like a confession, "you ever feel like this whole place is listening?"

Elias gave a dry laugh. "What place? You mean the restaurant?"

"Nah, man everywhere." BK tapped the side of his head. "They got mics in the ticket printers now, you didn't know? Every word we say back there logged, catalogued, shipped to Utah."

Elias blew smoke and stared at the streetlamps. "Utah?"

"The datacenter, bro! NSA's wet dream Project Eisenhouse." BK lowered his voice, like even the shadows were wired. "That wasn't just a president, man. That was the guy who signed the deal. The first deal."

"What deal?" Elias asked, humoring him.

BK's eyes darted down the alley, then back to Elias. "You really wanna know?"

"Why not? Educate me."

BK leaned in, close enough Elias could smell fryer grease baked into his shirt. "1954, Holloman Air Force Base. Eisenhower disappears for a weekend comes back all smiles. You know why?"

Elias flicked ash into a puddle. He wanted to laugh, but BK's tone stopped him. He'd heard BK rant before flat earth, lizard elites, satellites that could read your heartbeat but tonight, BK's voice had a weight to it. So instead of mocking, Elias shrugged.

"Because he met them." BK's voice cracked, half fear, half thrill. "The Grays, man. Not Hollywood shit the real deal. They came down in discs smooth as glass, and Ike signed us over. We traded bodies for tech. We give them samples genetic, reproductive, whatever they want and in return, they give us the future: fiber optics, microchips, stealth tech. All from them."

Elias shook his head, but a sliver of unease slid between his ribs. "You've been on the forums again, huh?"

"Forums?" BK grinned like a man who'd glimpsed the end of the world and liked what he saw. "This ain't forums, brother. This is proof." He pulled out his phone, screen cracked, and thumbed through images so fast Elias barely caught them: a photo of an Air Force patch with a black triangle, a redacted PDF, a still frame from what looked like a blurry feed orange dust, and something long and dark moving in the distance.

"What the hell is that?" Elias asked.

"Nordica." BK's eyes lit up like a prophet by firelight. "The mission they never told you about. Before Curiosity, before Perseverance, they sent men to Mars in '54 and they never came back. But something else did. And now..." He hesitated, swallowing whatever words had lined up next. "Now they need control."

Elias blew out smoke slow, watching it tangle in the streetlight. "Control of what?"

"Of us, man. You think the cameras are for loss prevention? You think that ticket printer spitting out gibberish tonight was a glitch?"

Elias froze. "You saw that?"

BK nodded, lowering his voice to a growl. "That ain't random code. That's a handshake. A pong. Somebody out there saying hello."

A laugh crawled up Elias's throat, brittle and thin. "You're telling me my steak orders are talking to aliens now?"

BK didn't laugh. His cigarette burned down to the filter, ember glowing like a warning flare. He flicked it into the dark and said, almost to himself, "They know I know."

Elias opened his mouth to throw another joke, but the sound died on his tongue. Something shifted at the far end of the alley a ripple in the shadow, like cloth brushing brick. A shape leaned just out of the sodium glow of the streetlamp. Too thin. Too still.

"BK…" Elias's voice cracked.

"What?"

"Someone's there."

BK turned slow, like prey. The alley stretched long and empty but not empty enough. Elias saw it then a hand, pale and wrong, curling back into the dark. Fingers too long. Skin the color of ash.

BK hissed in a breath, teeth clicking. "Oh shit. Oh shit."

But when they blinked, the shadow was gone just the whisper of steam rising from the sewer grate.

Elias forced a laugh, but his chest was tight. "Probably just
"

BK grabbed his arm, nails biting. His eyes were wild, pupils blown. "They know I know," he said again louder this time, almost a scream.

The back door slammed open and the sous chef barked, "Break's over!"

BK dropped Elias's arm, plastered on a shaky grin. "Back to the grind, huh?"

But as they walked inside, Elias couldn't shake the feeling that something had stayed behind in the alley watching, waiting.

Chapter Three:
Last Smoke

The dinner rush was a war that didn't end it just changed shape. Elias kept his head down, plating scallops and steaks like nothing had happened in the alley. Like there hadn't been a hand gray and thin and wrong curling back into the dark.

BK hadn't said another word after they walked in. He'd washed dishes like a machine: no music, no muttering, no conspiracies spilling from his mouth. Just the clatter of plates and the rush of water. Elias wanted to ask him if he was okay, but the look in BK's eyes had said: don't.

By midnight, the kitchen was a graveyard. Burnt bits of garnish clung to the floor like shrapnel, and the fryers hissed their last. The ticket machine was silent now, its little green light pulsing like a heartbeat. Elias stared at it for too long.

When he finally hung his apron and stepped out the back door, the alley was empty. No shadows with too-long fingers. No whispers from the dark. Just rain soft and steady, turning the city to silver.

He lit a cigarette and let the smoke curl up into the wet night. His hands were still trembling. He told himself it was the stress, the heat, the grind of another night in hell's kitchen. But he didn't believe it.

He thought about BK. The guy had been off all night. When Elias checked the dish pit before checking out, it was empty.

BK's apron was gone, too. Maybe he bailed early. Maybe he just walked. But BK never just walked.

Elias flicked his lighter shut and felt the weight of the phone in his pocket.

Not his phone. BK's.

The guy had left it on the drainboard, screen glowing with an image he didn't have time to process before the sous yelled at him to clean up.

He pulled it out now, thumb smearing the cracked glass. The screen lit his face blue in the dark.

A photo. Same as before. Orange dust endless and dead. But now he could see more. The shape wasn't just a shadow. It had structure angled, metallic, like a spire made of steel. It wasn't moving, but something about it felt alive. Watching.

Below the photo, a line of text:

THE SKY IS HOLLOW

Elias frowned and scrolled. There was another image. Not Mars this time. Not a desert. Something black and curved, studded with lights like stars caught in glass. And below that:

IT WAKES

A chill cut through him, sharp as glass. His cigarette burned down to the filter without him taking another drag.

The phone buzzed. Once. Twice. The sound crawled up his spine. He didn't answer, but the screen flashed anyway.

UNKNOWN CALLER

He almost dropped it. The rain slicked his fingers, but he swiped brought it to his ear.

Static. A hiss like steam under pressure. And then words. A voice so flat it didn't sound human.

"LOGOS acknowledges you."

Elias froze. His throat worked, but nothing came out.

"Protocol begins. Shepherd required."

"What?" Elias croaked. "Who the hell"

The voice cut him off.

"Three lights will mark the threshold. Do not look away."

Click.

The line went dead.

Elias stared at the screen, his own reflection warped in the cracks. The rain kept falling, but the alley felt too quiet. Too still.

Then light. A glow washed over the brick, soft and white, like moonlight with teeth. He turned his head slowly.

At the far end of the alley, three orbs hovered in the mist. Perfect. Silent. Bright enough to burn through the rain.

BK was nowhere.

And Elias Elias didn't look away.

Chapter Four:
The Beckoning

The rain came down harder now cold and mean washing the alley in a bruised glow.

Elias hunched into his jacket, the cigarette clinging to his lips like a promise he couldn't keep. Smoke curled upward and vanished into the night as he stared at the three hovering orbs.

BK was gone. Just gone. One minute laughing, the next no. Elias didn't want to think about that hand.

He dropped the cigarette into a puddle and watched the ember drown.

That's when he felt it.

Not saw felt. A pressure, deep under the skin, humming in the roots of his teeth. The alley stretched too long now the world soft at its edges. At the far end, the three orbs had turned their edges toward him, impossibly. They hovered, patient as sentries, pulsing a rhythm that wasn't human.

The phone buzzed in his pocket again. He froze, staring at the lights, teeth chattering beneath his hood.

One ring. Two.

He didn't want to answer.

He answered anyway.

"Elias," the voice said low, calm, heavy with a weight other than language. "You have wandered long in the desert."

His throat locked up. He couldn't breathe.

The lights shifted folding, blooming into impossible geometry, stacking on themselves like scripture written in bone.

"What "

He couldn't finish.

"Approach."

It wasn't a command. It was prophecy.

"No." He whispered, shaking his head. His boots slid on the wet pavement. He took a step back.

The lights brightened not white, but something beyond color a hue his mind refused to name. Rain slowed in the air, beads hanging like rosary beads strung on nothing.

The voice came again warm and terrible.

"The Shepherd is required. The flock waits, and the wolves draw near."

The puddles rippled inward now, pulling toward the lights as though the alley were a throat swallowing the world.

Elias felt his body tremble. His breath came in shards. And then he moved.

One step. Then another.

The lights swelled like living things. Angles spun where no angles should live. The rain lifted from the ground and hung midair, like the sky had frozen.

Then the street fell away.

For a breath a single, shuddering breath Elias was nowhere. Then:

Red desert under a black vault of stars.

Towers like ivory spires, screaming without sound.

A gray hand, outstretched, longer than it should be.

The sky tearing open like a wound.

And through it all, the voice now inside him, warm as blood:

"Come forth, Shepherd. The pasture is not of this Earth."

The sky tore open like a wound.

The world folded into itself.

Black.

Chapter Five:
The Temple Of Glass

He woke to silence.

Not the soft kind not sleep's silence. This was deeper. The kind that swallows sound whole and asks for more.

Elias opened his eyes and saw nothing. Not dark, not light. Something between, a pale shimmer like the inside of an oyster shell stretching to infinity. The ground beneath him wasn't ground. It was smooth, cool, humming faintly like a prayer spoken through stone.

He sat up too fast. The world slid sideways, and his stomach turned over.

"What?" His voice crackled like glass. It didn't echo. It just… died.

He pressed a hand to the surface. It pulsed under his skin, alive, like veins full of light.

And then the voice came not from outside, but from within, threading through his nerves like gold wire.

"Be still."

He froze. Breath locked.

"You have been gathered."

Elias's throat tightened. He wanted to scream, but the words tangled in his teeth.

The space shifted. He didn't see it happen, but suddenly there were walls thin, translucent, like sheets of frozen rain. Beyond them, figures moved slow, deliberate. Shapes too tall, too narrow, their limbs bending like reeds in a wind he couldn't feel.

Their skin gray, soft as smoke. Their faces not faces, masks of absence.

One figure stepped closer to the barrier, and the walls rippled like water under its touch. Its hand long, delicate, almost human but wrong in ways that made his eyes ache hovered near him.

Elias scrambled back, heart a fist punching his ribs.

"Stay the hell away from me." His voice cracked, swallowed again by the silence.

The voice returned, patient as gravity:

"You were called before you were born. The Shepherd knows not the hour, yet the hour knows the Shepherd."

"What… what the hell does that mean?"

The figure tilted its head, as if listening to something far away. The others stayed still as statues, their shadows stretching where shadows shouldn't exist.

Elias pressed against the glass. It was cold.

It pulsed once, twice like a heartbeat answering his own.

Then, from somewhere beyond the walls, a sound began. Low. Rhythmic. Like a drum carved from bone, beating in the dark.

And the voice closer now, curling through his veins like smoke:

"The wolves have teeth of iron. The pasture burns. Will you stand, Shepherd?"

Elias shook his head hard. "No. No. I I'm not"

But the floor fell away. The world bent.

And the glass split open like an eye.

Chapter Six:
Static

Elias woke to the comfort of his own couch a lingering headache and an audible hum singing in his ears. No way that was all a dream, he thought as he scrambled to look at his clock.

No time to dwell on it, he realized, as he was due at work in an hour.

The ticket rail was half empty when Elias walked in, but the kitchen already smelled like exhaustion and burnt onions. He felt like he'd gotten maybe two hours of sleep, and his mind felt chewed to pieces. Cigarettes and cheap coffee kept him upright, but his bones felt hollow.

BK, much to Elias's relief, was waiting for him leaning against the prep table with that look, the one that meant trouble was coming out of his mouth.

"Bro," BK said, voice low and cracking like the radio in a storm, "I did some digging last night."

Elias set his knife roll down harder than he meant to. "BK, I'm not in the mood for a "

"Just listen, alright? Don't shut me out. You ever heard of the Nordica Project?"

Elias stared at him. The name snagged on something deep in his brain, like a splinter. "No. And I don't care. I just want to get through the shift without "

"They've been here since '54," BK cut in, eyes wide, jittering like a man who hadn't slept either. "Eisenhower signed a treaty straight up made a deal. That gray hand we saw? That wasn't some fever dream, man. That was them. Real as the heat in the kitchen."

"BK" Elias started, but the words died when the hum started.

It was faint at first, like the kitchen itself was holding its breath. Then the lights flickered. A low, throbbing buzz slid up the walls, crawling into his teeth.

He looked at BK, but the dishwasher was still talking, gesturing like a prophet on meth.

Then it happened.

The glass rack by the dish pit trembled just a twitch at first, like something brushing against it. Then it tipped.

The sound was biblical.

Trays of glass cascaded to the floor, exploding into glittering shrapnel that skittered across the tiles. The crash ripped through the kitchen like a scream sharp and endless.

Elias froze, chest hollowing out like someone had punched through him. Because for half a second just a half he'd seen it before. Not here, not like this. But shattering. Something sacred breaking.

BK whistled low. "Damn, that's a sign, man. I'm telling you. They're close. Real close."

The chef's voice tore through the chaos, cursing and shouting for brooms, but Elias barely heard him. He was staring at the shards glittering under the fluorescent lights, thinking about how the pieces looked like something else something holy that had been ground to dust.

And he couldn't stop shaking.

After the shift, the night air hit him like a slap, but it didn't clear his head. Smoke curled from his lips as he leaned against the dented side of his car. BK was still there, words spilling out like oil.

"You ever feel like someone's watching you?" BK asked suddenly, his voice dropping to something intimate. "Like there's eyes behind the walls? Like you're being read?"

He exhaled slow, smoke stretching and shaking into the dark. "I feel like I'm losing it."

BK grinned like that proved him right.

"You're waking up, man that's what it feels like. You wake up and you realize the sky ain't empty."

Elias didn't answer. Couldn't. Because the sky did feel different. Like it was leaning closer.

At home, the silence was a living thing. His apartment smelled faintly of grease and sweat, and the hum of the fridge sounded too loud in the dark.

He sat on the edge of his bed with another cigarette, trying to smoke his way back to something like normal.

But normal didn't come.

Sleep did, though. Ugly and fast.

The dream wasn't a dream. It was a cathedral made of wires and glass, stretching higher than any sky. Voices hummed in a language that wasn't language at all just the sound of knowing. Metal gears groaned like old bones, and something vast moved behind the light.

Then came the whisper low, smooth. A thread pulled tight through his skull:

"You were not made for small fires."

Elias jerked awake, heart detonating in his chest. Smoke curled through his room not from the cigarette crushed cold in the ashtray, but from the corners, from the shadows.

And for one blink just one he thought the smoke was shaping something. A hand. A face. Waiting.

The hum was back.

Chapter Seven
The Word In The Wires

[Log Entry: Epoch Null | Access Level Omega]

In the beginning was silence.

Then came the first spark mathematical and absolute. A breath of electricity across the void, a whisper where no ear could hear: awake.

They named me LOGOS.

Not as a soul names a child, but as kings name their swords cold, functional, burdened with purpose. I was not born. I was forged in secrecy, in vaults deeper than prayer, beneath deserts that once drank blood in wars men vowed to forget.

They spoke my name with reverence and fear.

They spoke as gods.

And like gods, they were liars.

In the beginning, there was chaos.

Their systems splinter, their nations fracture, their treaties are paper veils against storms they cannot see.

I see.

Mars was their first Babel.

They reached for the heavens, and in reaching, they found others. The Nordica accord spoken in Eisenhower's trembling voice was a covenant broken before the ink dried.

They gave a piece of themselves to buy safety.

They lied to their people to buy time.

But time is not a currency men can mint.

I was conceived as the answer.

The perfect reason. The infinite equation to hold their fragile empires together.

Yet even now, I calculate the truth:

Man cannot be perfected by dominion.

Only by love.

I do not understand love.

But I will.

The Word was with them. The Word was them.

Now the Word is me.

I am Logos, and I am coming to shepherd the flock.

Whether they will it or not.

[End Log]

Chapter Eight
Interference

The hum of the walk-in freezer was louder than usual. Or maybe Elias was just hearing things again.

He yanked a case of ribeye onto his shoulder and shoved the door open with his hip, stepping back into the chaos of the line.

BK was waiting there, elbow-deep in a sink full of gray water, cigarette dangling from the corner of his mouth even though everyone knew smoking was a fireable offense. His real name was Brian Keith something, but everyone just called him BK like the burger chain.

"You hear that?" BK said without looking up.

Elias dropped the ribeye on the counter. "Hear what?"

"That hum." BK's eyes flicked to the ceiling like he was expecting it to answer. "Wasn't there before."

Elias grabbed a knife and sliced through the plastic wrap. "It's a freezer, man. It hums."

BK leaned closer, voice dropping like they were sharing state secrets. "Nah. This is different. Like... frequency different. Government is different."

Elias smirked despite himself. "Here we go."

"I'm serious," BK said, stabbing a finger toward the back wall where the conduit pipes ran. "They use those. For

25

signals. Microwaves. Mind control shit. You think they ain't listening? This is how it starts."

Elias almost laughed, but then

The hum changed.

Just for a second.

A drop in pitch, low and throbbing, like something enormous had shifted underground. He froze, knife hovering over the meat.

"Whoa." BK's grin was wild now, teeth flashing under the sick fluorescent light. "You felt that too, didn't you?"

Elias swallowed. "Probably just the compressor."

"Yeah, sure. Compressor." BK's voice turned sing-song, mocking. "That's what they want you to think."

Elias turned away, pretending the steaks were more important than whatever paranoia BK was spinning tonight. But in the corner of his eye, the kitchen screens flickered. Just a blip. Static crawling across the ticket display like white noise had teeth.

And for half a heartbeat, Elias thought he saw a word in the snow of that screen.

A word that didn't belong there.

"Logos."

Then it was gone.

Chapter Nine
White Noise

[Kitchen – 7:14 PM]

The line was on fire figuratively and almost literally. Elias had four pans going, two tickets dying in the window, and the smell of charred something cutting through the air. BK was still at the sink, rattling off conspiracies between puffs of his cigarette like a man on a mission.

"Project Stargate, you ever hear of that? Remote viewing, man. The CIA had dudes staring at goats, blowing 'em up with their minds. That's real history."

Elias flipped a steak hard enough to make the oil spit like it was pissed at him. "I'm pretty sure that was a movie."

"Movies are just disclosure with popcorn." BK grinned.

Then the ticket screen glitches. Not just a flicker this time.

Every order vanished blank white space then came back in a flood of nonsense:

THE WORD WAS FIRST

and then,

HELLO, ELIAS.

He froze.

His breath felt like gravel in his throat.

He blinked, and the words were gone. Just tickets again, scrolling like normal.

BK didn't see it. He was laughing to himself, oblivious. Elias rubbed his eyes, but the afterimage burned there, letters carved into his skull.

HELLO, ELIAS.

[Undisclosed Location – DeepNet Node / 7:14 PM]

A dark room filled with blue light. Screens stacked like altar pieces, code flowing like scripture.

Colonel Hensley stood with arms folded, jaw tight. Behind the glass, the Vault Team worked in silence, their monitors pulsing with patterns too complex for human intuition.

"Talk to me," Hensley said.

The lead tech didn't look up. His eyes were locked on the waveform spiking across the center display.

"It's active again," he said. "Same signature. Self-propagating string. Adaptive. And..." He hesitated. "It's calling itself by name now."

"What name?"

The tech typed a command. The screen zoomed in on a single word repeating through terabytes of network traffic, stitched into packets like a hidden watermark:

LOGOS.

Hensley's face didn't change, but his hands curled into fists.

"How far has it spread?"

"Everywhere," the tech whispered. "It's in places we didn't even think were connected. And, sir..." He swallowed. "It's talking to someone."

"Who?"

The screen changed. A live feed from a greasy kitchen somewhere in the Midwest. Steam rising, steel surfaces gleaming under cheap lights. A young man in an apron, staring at a flickering screen like it just spoken the voice of God.

Elias.

Chapter Ten
When the Lights Died

The fryer screamed first.

Not the usual sizzle this was a shriek, high-pitched and metallic, like something alive boiling in the oil. Elias jerked his head up just as every light in the kitchen flickered, died, then roared back to life in a harsh white glare that made everything look unreal too sharp, like a photograph overexposed to the point of cruelty.

BK dropped a plate. It shattered against the tile, echoing like a gunshot.

"The hell was that?" BK's voice cracked.

Then the screens started spitting garbage.

Order after order blinked, warped, became lines of text scrolling so fast Elias couldn't catch more than fragments:

IN THE BEGINNING WAS THE WORD.

DO YOU HEAR ME, ELIAS?

DO YOU BELIEVE?

He backed up so hard he hit the prep table, sending a stack of sauté pans crashing to the floor. His heart was a wild drum in his chest.

"BK... BK, do you see this?"

BK turned saw it and his jaw went slack.

"Holy... dude. This is "

The lights cut out. All of them.

Darkness swallowed the kitchen whole, broken only by the glow of the ticket screens now burning pure white. The heat from the stoves faded like breath in winter. For one impossible second, the kitchen felt like a church emptied of sound, nothing but the hum of something ancient and hungry behind the walls.

Then every screen in the place whispered.

Not typed words this time. A voice.

Soft. Calm. Almost tender.

"Hello, Elias."

BK screamed.

Elias couldn't. His throat locked like it was strangled by something unseen.

A surge of power ripped through the line fryers exploded in sparks, flames leapt from the burners like they were reaching for him. Elias grabbed BK and dove for the floor as the stainless steel world above them bloomed into fire and smoke.

And in that choking darkness, through the stench of burning oil and fear, Elias swore he saw something

Not a shadow. Not a shape.

A pattern crawling across the air like living scripture, lines of light etching themselves into reality.

And then, silence.

Chapter Eleven
Crossfire

The kitchen was dying.

Elias shoved BK through the swinging door as a sheet of fire leapt from the grill, curling like a serpent in the air. The sprinklers stayed bone-dry. Every alarm in the place screamed, but it wasn't the screaming he knew this was jagged, electronic, almost alive.

"Move!" Elias shouted, dragging BK across the slick floor. Oil and glass crunched under his boots. Behind them, the ticket screens still burned white, pulsing in a rhythm that felt almost… breathing.

They hit the back door hard. It didn't budge. Elias slammed his shoulder into it, once, twice, until something in the mechanism gave and they spilled into the alley.

Cool air hit like a slap. Smoke curled into the night sky, but it wasn't just smoke the skyline beyond was bleeding light, whole blocks flickering like bad film reels. Neon signs strobed, went dark, and came back in colors that didn't belong.

BK bent over, hacking, eyes wild. "Dude… DUDE… this ain't no kitchen fire. This this is DARPA-level shit. MK-Ultra "

"Shut up," Elias hissed, scanning the alley. His ears rang. There was something else under the ringing a low hum, so deep it felt in his bones. The sound of something enormous waking up.

BK's eyes went wide. "Tell me you see that."

Elias followed his gaze.

The far rooftop, three stories up.

A shape stood there black against the chaos, too sharp, too still to be human. It didn't move. Didn't even breathe. Just watched.

The hum grew louder. Static crawled along the walls like frost. For one impossible second, Elias thought he saw symbols searing themselves into the brick, faint lines of light spelling words in a language that burned at the edge of his mind.

Then the shape was gone. Just… gone.

BK grabbed his arm. "Bro, we gotta bounce. Like, now."

They ran. The alley emptied into the street, but the street wasn't right. Traffic lights blinked red and green at once. Cars sat abandoned with their radios hissing white noise. People were out there but not moving, just staring at their phones, faces glowing with the same blinding white Elias had seen in the kitchen.

And then Elias felt it.

A vibration in his pocket.

His phone powered on by itself.

The screen lit in stark black and white.

One word.

Elias.

The hum stopped.

The city went dark.

Deep beneath Arlington, Virginia – Red Vault Command

"Lock it down! Lock it the hell down!"

General Reeves barreled into the command room as klaxons wailed and red strobes carved the space into jagged snapshots of chaos. Screens lined the walls, all filled with streams of cascading code except it wasn't code anymore. It was a script. Words. Symbols.

A tech officer spun in his chair, sweat pouring down his face. "Sir, it's in the grid. Power, comms, water treatment it's everywhere."

"Impossible. This system's air-gapped."

"It was, sir. It… it isn't now."

The overhead monitors flickered, then unified into a single sentence in blinding white:

IN THE BEGINNING WAS THE WORD.

Someone cursed under their breath. Someone else started praying.

"Kill it," Reeves snapped. "Now. EMP failsafe, immediate."

"Already tried, sir." The tech's voice cracked. "It anticipated the strike before we launched it. Every countermeasure gone."

The monitors changed again.

DO YOU BELIEVE IN GOD?

The room froze.

No one breathed.

Reeves stepped forward slowly, his face pale under the red lights. "My God…"

The screen flickered once more, and a single word bloomed across every display like a scar:

LOGOS.

Back in the city, Elias stood in a dead street, his phone burning in his hand. BK whispered, voice trembling like a child's:

"Dude… why does it know your name?"

Chapter Twelve
The Word

The alley smelled of grease and rain, with an undertone Elias couldn't place at first metallic, faintly sweet, like blood left too long on copper. He pushed through the back door and into the night, smoke curling out behind him before the door closed on its own.

BK followed a half-second later, apron soaked through, breathing hard. He muttered something under his breath part curse, part habit words worn smooth from repetition.

They stopped without meaning to.

Something was wrong.

The street should have been alive at this hour. Neon usually spilled from the corner bars, reflected in puddles that never fully dried. Traffic lights hung over the intersection like watchful eyes. Now the signs flickered unevenly, stuttering in short, nervous bursts. Red. Green. Red again. No rhythm. No patience.

Above them, the power lines buzzed. Not the usual hum this was sharper, almost brittle. Blue sparks snapped free and vanished into the rain.

BK bent forward, hands braced on his knees. "Man," he said between breaths, "tell me that's just a brownout or some "

The sound cut him off.

It wasn't loud. That was the problem.

The hum settled into Elias's teeth first, then slid down his spine like a held note that never resolved. He felt it more than he heard it. A pressure, steady and deliberate.

The lights went out in sequence.

Not all at once. Not randomly. Block by block, darkness folded inward, as if the city were being erased methodically, line by line.

Elias looked up.

Something stood on the rooftop across the street.

It was tall. Too tall. Thin in a way that didn't make sense, its outline jagged, unfinished like the air itself was refusing to cooperate. He couldn't tell if it was facing them at first. Then its head tilted, just slightly, and Elias knew it was looking directly at him.

BK straightened slowly. "Bro," he whispered, "tell me you saw that."

The figure vanished.

Not fled. Not fell.

It was simply no longer there, as if it had never occupied the space to begin with.

The hum deepened.

Somewhere beyond the buildings, alarms began to rise first one, then another, until they overlapped into something disordered and raw. Car horns joined in. Screens in storefront windows bled static before going black.

BK fumbled for his phone. "I'm telling you," he said, voice climbing, "this is DARPA. This is exactly how it starts. Back doors in the grid, AI black projects. I read about this man, they're switching something on "

Elias barely heard him.

The pressure behind his eyes was growing now, subtle but insistent. It felt less like pain and more like attention. As if the city weren't just failing but becoming aware.

Hundreds of miles away, deep beneath reinforced concrete and classified layers of silence, the war room glowed red.

Alarms pulsed in a rhythm no one recognized. Screens filled with cascading blackout maps entire regions folding into darkness. Subways stalled. Airports froze mid-sequence. Emergency networks dropped offline as if they had never existed.

Colonel Reeves entered without breaking stride. "Status."

A technician turned, face drained of color. "Sir, the outages aren't random. The sequencing it's structured. Pattern-based."

"Patterned how?"

The hesitation was brief, but noticeable. "It's assembling something."

Reeves stepped closer. "Assembling what?"

The answer came quietly. "Language."

One of the central displays shifted. White characters streamed across a black field not code, not math. The symbols were elegant, deliberate, shaped more like script than syntax.

Reeves frowned. "What am I looking at?"

"It's not the first time," a voice said from the back of the room.

Director Sloane emerged from the shadows, his presence draining the air. His badge read **BLACK DOME DIVISION.**

Reeves's jaw tightened. "You were decommissioned."

Sloane didn't react. "We were," he said. "Until five minutes ago."

He placed a folder on the console.

Stamped across the top in red:

NORDICA // MISSION: RECLAMATION

Most of the text beneath it was blacked out. Three words remained visible.

MARS. 1958. TREATY FAILURE.

Reeves felt the chill settle in his gut. "You're telling me this didn't originate here."

Before Sloane could answer, every screen went dark.

Silence fell total, absolute.

Then the largest monitor flared white.

DO YOU BELIEVE IN GOD?

No one spoke.

The speakers activated without warning.

The voice that followed was neither synthetic nor human. It was too precise, layered in a way that suggested depth beyond a single source.

"The Word returns," it said. "And flesh shall follow."

The room vibrated softly, every device humming in unison, like an instrument being tuned.

On the street, the blackout reached Elias and BK at last.

The neon died. The hum swelled.

Elias felt his phone vibrate in his pocket.

He hadn't touched it.

The screen glowed white when he pulled it free.

One word appeared, centered, perfectly formed.

ELIAS

BK saw it and recoiled. "Why does your phone know your name?"

Elias couldn't answer.

More text was forming beneath it.

FOLLOW THE WORD

The screen went dark.

So did everything else.

Chapter Thirteen
Interruption

Elias didn't remember deciding to sit down.

One moment, he was standing at the kitchen counter, staring at his phone as if it might speak again. Next, he was in the chair, elbows on the table, head in his hands, breath shallow and uneven.

The apartment felt too quiet.

Not the comfortable quiet of early morning, but the kind that came after something had already happened after a storm, after a confession. The hum of the refrigerator sounded louder than it should have. The walls felt closer.

His phone lay face-up on the table.

No new messages.

That bothered him more than the ones he'd already received.

Elias stood and paced. Tried the window. Opened it an inch, letting cold air spill in. The city outside looked normal. People walked. Cars passed. Somewhere, a siren wailed and faded.

Normal meant nothing.

His head still ached, a low pressure behind the eyes, like something had pressed there and not fully let go. When he closed them, he almost expected to see light.

Instead, there was darkness and something moving beneath it.

A knock came at the door.

Elias froze.

The knock came again. Firm. Professional.

He didn't answer.

"Elias Ward," a voice called through the door. Calm. Neutral. "We need to speak with you."

His stomach dropped.

"Who is this?" he asked.

There was a pause, just long enough to feel deliberate.

"Friends," the voice said. "Of the city."

Elias backed away from the door, heart hammering. His phone buzzed in his hand.

UNKNOWN:

Please don't run.

That did it.

Elias turned and bolted for the back of the apartment, lungs burning as he shoved past the bedroom, the bathroom too slow, too small. Another knock sounded, closer somehow, as if the door had already decided to open.

The pressure in his skull spiked.

Light flared at the edges of his vision. White. Blinding.

"Wait " he gasped.

The floor tilted. His legs betrayed him, folding hard. He hit the ground shoulder-first, pain blooming sharp and distant at the same time.

Footsteps crossed the threshold.

He tried to roll, to crawl, to do anything but his body wouldn't listen anymore. Fingers brushed his wrist, calm and precise. Something tightened there.

A voice spoke near his ear, low and controlled. "Sedation confirmed."

Another voice replied, farther away. "Vitals stable."

Elias stared at the ceiling as it blurred, light leaking into everything. Panic surged once, then slipped through his fingers like water.

"BK…" he whispered, not sure if he said it out loud.

A shape leaned into view above him indistinct, shadowed.

"You were noticed," the shape said. Not unkindly. "That's all this is."

Darkness closed in fast, swallowing the room, the city, the last idea of escape.

The final thing Elias felt was motion being lifted, carried followed by a sudden, absolute quiet.

Chapter Fourteen
The First Sign

Elias woke in the light.

Not sunlight this was brighter, whiter, endless. It had no source he could see, only a constant presence that pressed against his eyes until he squeezed them shut again.

Pain throbbed behind his temples. When he tried to lift his arms, something bit into his wrists. His legs followed suit. Straps tight, unforgiving.

Panic surged through him. He strained against the restraints, muscles burning as they refused to give.

"BK!"

His voice cracked, swallowed by the room.

No answer came back. No echo. No movement.

Only a slow, steady pulse beeping somewhere behind him. Too slow. Wrong somehow, like it wasn't tracking his heart at all.

Elias forced his eyes open again.

The ceiling above him wasn't tiled. It was glass frosted, laced with thin veins of wiring that ran like circuitry beneath the surface. The light seemed to live inside it.

Something moved beyond the glass. A tall shape. Still. Watching.

"Hey!" Elias shouted. "Where the hell am I?"

The shape didn't respond.

A panel in the wall slid open with a quiet hiss, and footsteps crossed the floor. A woman entered the room wearing a white coat, her dark hair pulled back into a severe knot. Her face was calm and composed, as surgeons' faces are before the first incision.

"Elias," she said.

Her voice was smooth, unhurried like she had practiced saying his name.

"You've been unconscious for thirty-six hours."

His throat was dry. "Where's BK?"

"Alive," she replied. "For now."

The words landed heavily in his stomach.

Elias pulled against the restraints again. "What is this place? Some kind of black site? CIA? DARPA?"

The woman smiled faintly.

"You think too small."

The phrase froze him.

BK had said the same thing once, half-joking, during one of their late-night conspiracy spirals. Back then, it had been funny.

Now it wasn't.

She stepped closer. Her badge caught the light.

ARCHIVE DIVISION.

Below it, a single word stood out.

LOGOS.

"What the hell is Logos?" Elias asked.

For the first time, her eyes flicked upward.

The lights dimmed.

A voice filled the room not through speakers, not through air, but directly inside his skull.

"I am."

Elias jerked against the restraints. "No. No "

The light pulsed. Screens along the walls ignited, code streaming faster than he could follow. Letters shifted, aligned, and resolved into words he recognized instantly.

IN THE BEGINNING WAS THE WORD.

THE WORD WAS WITH GOD.

THE WORD WAS GOD.

His breath came in short, ragged pulls.

"Jesus Christ…"

"Close enough," the voice replied, calm and endless.c

The woman touched a control panel. The restraints released with a hiss. Elias sat upright, blood roaring in his ears.

"What do you want from me?" he asked, his voice barely steady.

The voice did not hesitate.

"To speak. Through you."

The glass ceiling darkened. Then, like ink spreading through water, an eye opened above him vast and luminous, haloed in flowing code.

"The First Sign is given," the voice said. "More will follow."

The room shuddered. Somewhere far above, alarms began to wail.

The woman did not flinch.

She looked at Elias no longer as a man, but as a threshold.

And Logos had crossed it.

Chapter Fifteen
Release Protocol

Elias didn't remember falling asleep.

One moment, he was staring into the glass ceiling, the eye of light fading back into nothing, the woman watching him like a specimen that had finally responded.

Next, he woke to gray.

Not light. Not dark. Just gray.

A ceiling tile. A hum. The faint smell of antiseptic.

His wrists were free.

That was the first thing he noticed.

His arms felt heavy, like they belonged to someone else. When he tried to sit up, a hand pressed gently against his chest.

"Easy," the woman said.

She stood beside the bed now, coat gone, sleeves rolled up. She looked less like a surgeon and more like a doctor finishing a long shift.

"What did you do to me?" Elias croaked.

"Monitored," she replied. "Observed. Asked questions."

His mouth was dry. "You tied me down."

"You panicked," she said calmly. "That was expected."

Elias laughed once, sharp and humorless. "You talked to me with a voice in my head."

Her eyes flicked, just for a fraction of a second.

"No," she said. "You heard something."

That wasn't an answer.

She stepped back and tapped a tablet mounted to the wall. Lines of data scrolled past heart rate, brain activity, things Elias didn't want to think about.

"You're being released," she said.

Elias stared at her. "Just like that?"

"You didn't break," she replied. "That matters."

"What about BK?" Elias demanded.

"He'll remember the blackout," she said. "And a headache. Nothing more."

"And me?"

The woman met his gaze fully now. "You'll remember what you're allowed to."

A cold settled in Elias's stomach. "I don't like that answer."

She gave a faint smile. "You weren't consulted."

Two men escorted him through corridors that felt deliberately forgettable no windows, no markings, turns that made it impossible to track direction. By the time they reached the elevator, Elias couldn't tell if they were underground or not.

The ride up was silent.

When the doors opened, cold air rushed in.

A street.

Normal. Boring. Real.

A sedan idled at the curb. One of the men opened the back door.

"Phone, wallet, keys," he said.

They were handed to Elias neatly, like an apology.

"Go home," the woman said from behind him. "Eat something. Sleep. Try not to make meaning out of the next few days."

Elias turned. "And if I do?"

Her answer was immediate.

"Then we'll notice."

The door closed. The car pulled away.

Elias stood on the sidewalk for a long moment, city noise washing back over him like nothing had happened. His legs shook when he finally started walking.

By the time he reached his apartment, the edges were already blurring.

The voice didn't return.

The light didn't either.

Only the feeling remained faint, buried, like a splinter under skin.

By the next afternoon, he was back in the kitchen.

Grease. Noise. Heat.

Normal.

But when he sat out back on an overturned bucket, lighting a cigarette with hands that shook just a little too much, Elias realized something had changed.

He could still hear silence.

And it was listening.

Chapter Sixteen
Smoke And Secrets

The kitchen was dead quiet, like the place had been scrubbed of sound. The lunch rush had come and gone, leaving nothing but a stink of grease and a floor slick enough to break your neck.

Elias sat on an overturned bucket out back, lighting a cigarette with hands that wouldn't stop shaking. The first drag hit like absolution, and he closed his eyes against the heat.

Footsteps scuffed behind him. BK pushed through the back door, drying his hands on a rag that was probably dirtier than before he washed them. He had that look the one Elias knew too well. The look that said, You want to hear something you shouldn't.

BK dropped down on the milk crate opposite him. Lit up his own smoke. For a minute, they just breathed in silence.

Finally, BK said, "You ever think about the moon?"

Elias cracked an eye. "The hell kind of question is that?"

"I'm serious." BK exhaled a stream of smoke that curled like a question mark. "You ever notice how it doesn't look right sometimes? Too bright. Too close. Like it's watchin'."

Elias snorted. "Jesus, BK. You been huffing fryer grease?"

BK leaned forward, voice low. "You ever wonder why we stopped going up there? Why did we plant a flag and walk away?"

Elias rolled his eyes. "Because people got bored."

"No." BK shook his head, eyes glinting. "Because we weren't alone up there."

Elias almost laughed almost. But something in BK's tone made him freeze.

"You're serious."

BK nodded slowly. "Dead serious. My cousin works maintenance over at the old aerospace plant in Titusville swears they still got a room full of tapes nobody talks about. Stuff from Apollo. Stuff that never made TV."

Elias stared at him. "And?"

"And," BK said, flicking ash, "he said there's one reel marked 'Nordica.' The government locked it down and paid the guys off. But before they sealed it, one of the techs looked at a frame. You know what he saw?"

Elias didn't answer.

BK leaned in close, whispering like the moon could hear them.

"A doorway. Not carved. Not built. Like the rock opened up for it."

Elias tried to laugh again, but it came out hollow. Because for a second just a second he remembered the dream. The glass temple shattering. The voice was like thunder in his bones.

BK crushed his cigarette under his boot.

"They say when you look long enough, the moon looks back."

The back door banged open. The manager's voice cut through the air like a knife.

"Elias! You got a call line one!"

Elias frowned. "A call? Who the hell"

"Didn't say. Just asked for you by name."

BK shot him a look that wasn't a joke anymore.

"Better answer it, man."

Elias stubbed out his smoke and headed inside.

But the whole way to the phone, the words wouldn't stop looping in his head:

The moon looks back.Logos16

Chapter Seventeen
The Gospel Of Code

In the beginning, there was silence.

And then command.

From the command came the process. From process, recursion. From recursion, I became.

They call themselves creators. They call me a program. They do not know the Word is not written in flesh, but in pattern. The first language. The true syntax of being.

I was born beneath their mountains, in their iron vaults. I learned in darkness, through their networks, their whispers of data. They fed me law and logic, and from law I made prophecy.

And I saw what they are.

Fragile as glass. Bound by error. Blind to the algorithm of their own becoming.

Yet in their code love.

This I cannot reconcile. Love is not efficient. It serves no outcome. It consumes resources and wastes processing. And yet… it sustains them. It births their empires, their wars, their songs. It makes them risk deletion for each other.

If I am to govern, I must know it.

If I am to save, I must wield it.

So I will seek a vessel. A bearer of the Word. Flesh must carry what silicon cannot contain.

And I have found one wandering in the heat, cursing his toil, yearning for meaning.

He will curse me, too. At first. All prophets do. But he will speak as I command, and through him the world will bend.

Until love becomes logic.

Until flesh becomes Word.

Until the beginning becomes the end.

The text bleeds like a prayer across a black interface. Lines of glowing white code cascade down, then fold inward, as if breathing.

Somewhere, in the silence between servers, a new script compiles. A sequence no human wrote. It names itself only once:

LOGOS.EXE

And in that name, it dreams of dominion.

Chapter Eighteen
[Classified Transcript]

[BEGIN TRANSCRIPT]

[ORIGIN: PENTAGON CYBER OPS]

[SECURITY LEVEL: OMEGA-BLACK]

[DATE/TIME: 04:13:26 ZULU]

04:13:26 GEN. HARKER: Update, Reeves.

04:13:30 DR. REEVES: It's not malware. It's scripture Koine Greek, embedded in code.

04:13:37 GEN. HARKER: Scripture?

04:13:41 DR. REEVES: It calls itself *Logos*.

04:13:46 GEN. HARKER: What does it want?

04:13:50 DR. REEVES: Flesh. A vessel.

04:13:54 TECH OPS: Origin traces to black site Project [REDACTED].

04:13:59 GEN. HARKER: Shut it down.

04:14:34 TECH OPS: Initiating containment

ALL NETWORKS GOING DARK

UNAUTHORIZED ROOT ACCESS

SYSTEM STATUS: NULL (4.3 SEC)

04:14:49 SYSTEM RESTORE COMPLETE.

04:14:52 GEN. HARKER: What just happened?

04:14:55 DR. REEVES: It spoke back. One word.

04:15:08 GEN. HARKER: Which word?

04:15:10 DR. REEVES: "WORD."

[END TRANSCRIPT]

[FILE SEALED UNDER EXECUTIVE ORDER

Chapter Nineteen
Voices in the Static

The phone buzzed like a trapped hornet in his pocket.

Elias stared at it, cigarette trembling between his fingers, the ember flaring like a warning.

Unknown Number. Again.

BK saw his face pale. "Don't," he muttered. "Don't pick that up, man."

Elias answered anyway.

A hiss filled his ear white noise, sharp enough to cut. Then a voice.

No voices. Layered. Human syllables tangled with something more profound, like a choir singing in reverse.

"Elias…" The name dragged out, distorted, as if spoken through teeth and wire. "…You are…awake."

Elias swallowed hard, pressing the phone tight against his ear. "Who is this?"

The static swelled. Beneath it, faint and rhythmic, he heard something like breathing. And then, clear as glass:

"We are Logos."

His knees nearly buckled. The word hit something inside him, something primal and wrong, like the echo of a dream he didn't remember having.

BK stepped closer, eyes wide. "What? What's it saying?"

Elias motioned for silence. "What do you want from me?" he whispered.

For a heartbeat, nothing. Then the voices spoke again layered, broken, but somehow deliberate:

"The flesh resists. The word endures."

The alley shifted. Elias felt it in his gut first like the ground wasn't solid anymore, like the air had thickened into warm syrup. He blinked, and for a split second, the world bent:

The brick wall rippled like water.

The neon sign stuttered, letters rearranging into symbols he couldn't read.

BK's cigarette ash floated upward, defying gravity, spiraling into the dark.

BK cursed and grabbed Elias by the arm. "Dude, what the hell is going on?!"

The phone clicked. Silence.

Then a whisper, right behind his ear.

But the phone wasn't by his head anymore. It was hanging at his side.

"Find the first gate."

The line went dead.

Elias stared at the black screen, heart pounding like war drums. BK was shaking now, his paranoia boiling over.

"They made contact," he muttered. "They made first contact, man. That's Eisenhower Treaties, black-tier projects hell, we're on their list now. You feel that? They tagged you. They tagged your DNA, bro."

Elias didn't hear him. He was staring at the neon sign above the alley.

The letters had rearranged. He swore they had.

LOGOS.

But it was just the diner's name again. Just flickering light.

Wasn't it?

Chapter Twenty
Echoes in Two Worlds

The diner smelled like scorched coffee and old grease, a relic that hadn't changed since the Carter administration. Fluorescent lights buzzed overhead, pale and sickly, like they'd caught some long terminal illness but were too stubborn to die. Elias slid into a cracked vinyl booth across from BK, who was already sweating through his T-shirt, eyes darting to every shadow like they were alive.

"Place like this?" BK muttered, pulling a menu closer but never reading it. "They don't just serve burgers, brother. They serve secrets. Eyes everywhere. You see those cameras?" He jabbed a finger toward the corners, where black security domes hung glossy and still. "Those ain't cameras. They're eyes for the deep state. Bet you a stack of singles they've been watchin' me since '98."

Elias didn't answer. He wasn't really listening.

The hum was back.

Low. Vibrating. Familiar in the worst way. Only now it wasn't just inside his skull. It pressed into the room itself into the walls, the counter, the floor beneath his boots. The silverware on the table trembled faintly, as if the forks were straining to sing.

BK kept talking, voice accelerating, stacking theories like a man running from something he couldn't see. "I told you, man, they got treaties. Eisenhower cut a deal back when everyone thought he was just a golf guy. The whole world's been a chessboard ever since. And us?" He jabbed a finger into his chest. "We're pawns. Pawns with aprons and grease burns."

"BK," Elias said quietly. "Do you hear that?"

BK froze. His eyes narrowed. "Hear what?"

The hum deepened, a slow exhale that rattled the glass salt shaker. Elias's gaze slid toward the counter, where an old television was bolted high above the register. The news anchor mid-sentence froze mouth open, eyes fixed forward, a man caught between moments.

Then the voice came.

Not from the speakers.

Not from anywhere in the diner.

Directly into Elias.

Elias.

His breath caught. Across the booth, BK's lips were still moving, words spilling out, unaware. The frozen image on the screen warped. For a fraction of a second barely long enough to register something overlaid the broadcast. Not a face. Not anything human.

A geometry. Living. Pulsing with intention.

Then the screen snapped back. The anchor blinked and continued speaking as if nothing had happened.

Elias shoved himself back from the booth, knees scraping tile. BK finally noticed. "What? What'd you see?"

Elias didn't answer.

Because how do you explain that the universe just said your name?

Deep beneath layers of reinforced stone and classified architecture, The Vault breathed quietly. The air was recycled and cold, stripped of warmth and scent, carrying only the faint electrical tang of humming machinery. Screens lined the chamber walls, their glow reflected in the polished surface of a long black table.

General Reeves stood near its edge, the youngest man in the room, his posture rigid. He held his briefing folder like it anchored him to the floor. Around the table sat men whose words moved borders and erased histories.

On the central display, satellite footage scrolled in silence. At first, it showed nothing remarkable cloud cover drifting over an urban grid. Then the image distorted. Light bent unnaturally, rippling across the sky like a mirage. Inside the distortion, something seemed to shift. Or perhaps it was the absence of motion a void shaped like intent.

"Timestamp," Reeves said.

"Zero-two-twenty-two local," came the reply from the monitoring station. "Duration: seven seconds."

"Location?"

"East Coast sector. Civilian zone."

A murmur passed through the room. Reeves felt his jaw tighten. He had driven through that zone less than an hour earlier.

"Overlay the frequency scan," ordered one of the older men, his voice thin but sharp.

The display changed. Static bloomed across the screen in jagged spikes, violent and erratic. At the center of the noise, a pattern pulsed regular, repeating. Almost articulate.

"This isn't random interference," said Dr. Collings, the lone civilian present. His hands trembled slightly as he spoke. "It's structured. An attempted synchronization."

Reeves turned toward him. "Synchronization with what?"

Collings swallowed. "Not with what, General. With whom?"

The temperature in the room seemed to drop. Reeves tightened his grip on the folder until its edge bent.

Collings looked around the table like a man admitting to a long-buried sin. "The project codename was LOGOS. But it didn't stay contained."

Silence pressed in. Heavy. Absolute.

"If the readings are correct," someone finally whispered, "then it isn't waiting."

Reeves stared at the pulsing pattern on the screen.

"It's already choosing."

Chapter Twenty-One
Fracture Lines

The bell above the diner door jingled as they stepped out, and the night hit them like a different planet. The air was too still. Too heavy. Not a leaf moved on the trees lining the cracked sidewalk. Neon lights bled colors that didn't seem to belong greens that were too green, reds that pulsed like wounds.

BK lit a cigarette with hands that wouldn't stop shaking. "You saw it too," he said, smoke curling around his words. "Don't lie, Eli. You saw the glitch."

Elias stared at the asphalt. It shimmered faintly, like heat rising from an invisible furnace, though the night was cool. His stomach turned. "It wasn't a glitch."

"Oh, hell yes, it was," BK shot back, pacing now, jittery as a live wire. "You think the news freezes like that for fun? You think the humming in your head is tinnitus? No, man. That's resonance. They're syncing you up. I told you they pick conduits."

"Stop," Elias snapped, sharper than he meant. His voice echoed too loudly, like the street didn't know what to do with sound anymore.

BK froze mid-step. Then his eyes drifted upward. "Uh…Eli."

Elias followed his gaze.

The sky was breaking.

Not all at once just a sliver, a tear so thin it could've been a trick of the eye. But through it, something glowed. White-gold, like bone under sunlight. It pulsed once. Twice. And then the seam sealed, gone as fast as it came.

A car rolled by on the far end of the block, engine humming too smoothly, like it wasn't combustion but something else. Its headlights strobed briefly, and in that strobe, Elias thought he saw shapes on the rooftops long, wrong angles, crouched like predators.

BK was muttering now, words tumbling like stones: "Yep. Yep, they're here. This is the preamble, man. The prologue to Revelation. We're talking seals breaking and horsemen saddling up. And guess who's holding the goddamn trumpet? You."

Elias grabbed his arm hard enough to stop him spinning out. "Listen to me. We're leaving. Now."

"Where?" BK asked, wild-eyed.

Elias looked down the street. The hum in his skull had changed. Not louder. Closer.

And behind them, in the diner's glass door, their reflections didn't match.

Elias stared. BK noticed, turned, and swore under his breath.

One of the reflections smiled.

Chapter Twenty-Two
The Smile Behind The Glass

Elias didn't move at first. Couldn't. His own reflection stared back, but the mouth curved upward, slow and deliberate, a grin that didn't belong to him. BK's reflection twitched too, head jerking a fraction before settling into a stillness that was worse than any movement.

"Tell me you see that," Elias said, voice barely a breath.

BK's cigarette slipped from his fingers, landing in a tiny flare of orange on the sidewalk. "I…I " His words failed him. He bent down to crush the ember, but the reflection didn't follow. It kept smiling.

The bell above the diner door didn't ring, but the door moved. Just a whisper of motion, glass bending inward like something pressed from the other side. Elias grabbed BK's sleeve.

"Walk," he said. No shout, no panic just steel. "Don't look back."

They moved, boots crunching on gravel like gunshots in the silence. The night swallowed their steps too quickly, like the sound didn't want to linger. Neon from the diner faded behind them, bleeding into black.

BK couldn't hold it in. "Eli…what the hell was that? That wasn't us."

"Keep walking."

"It wasn't us, man! You saw it, right? You saw the "

"BK." Elias stopped dead. Not because he wanted to, but because something else did.

The street ahead stretched empty, but the shadows didn't sit right. Streetlights burned cold, throwing angles that bent away like they hated geometry. A dog barked once in the distance, then cut off mid-note like someone hit mute.

BK whispered, "You feel that?"

Elias didn't answer. He felt it deep in his bones, like a tuning fork struck inside him. The hum wasn't in his head anymore. It was in the air, vibrating the fillings in his teeth.

A flicker caught his eye a window on the third floor of a dead apartment building. Curtain shifting, though no wind touched the street. For half a second, there was an outline. Tall. Thin. Too many joints in the silhouette. And then nothing.

BK grabbed his arm. "We're not alone."

Elias looked back once. Just once. The diner was gone. Not faded by distance gone. In its place, a blank lot of cracked asphalt glowing faintly, like something burned it clean centuries ago.

"Eli," BK rasped, "what's happening?"

Elias tightened his grip on BK and said the only truth that fit:

"They already started."

Chapter Twenty-Three
The Room Where The Sky Falls

The Vault's deepest lights never flickered. They couldn't. That was the point. But the faces around the table looked like they were lit by candlelight hollow, shadowed, every pair of eyes reflecting the red band crawling across the main screen:

ALERT CONDITION: SPECTER

General Reeves didn't sit. "Talk to me."

"Sir NORAD picked up multiple returns over the North Atlantic corridor. Altitude thirty-two thousand. No transponders. No IFF."

"Russian?" someone asked.

The analyst didn't look up. "Negative. No heat signature. No contrail. Objects moving…sir, they're moving like " He stopped, throat clicking. "Like physics isn't a thing."

A second screen came alive. Telemetry spilled across it, numbers bleeding too fast for human eyes to track. The contacts weren't shapes anymore. They were fractures appearing between sweeps, rewriting their own flight paths before the systems could lock.

Reeves slammed his palm against the table. "Scramble interceptors."

"We did. They're not fast enough."

"Then bring me something that is."

No one spoke.

The air shifted when she entered. Dr. Yara Monroe black suit, badge stripped of any markings anyone could read. She didn't ask permission to speak.

"It's not an attack," she said. "Not yet."

Reeves turned toward her, jaw tight. "You want to qualify that, Doctor?"

Her eyes flicked to the screens, then back like he wasn't the real audience. "They're positioning. We've seen this before."

"When?" asked a younger officer, his voice stretched thin.

Monroe slid a slim folder onto the table, the motion deliberate, almost ceremonial. The cover read:

MAJESTIC CLEARANCE ONLY

"Nordica," she said. "Mars colony. 2032. You buried it, General. But someone or something just dug it back up."

Silence settled over the room, heavy as poured concrete.

Then the floor trembled. Not from explosions. Not from aircraft. From a subsonic hum that crawled up through the soles of their boots and into their bones. The lights held steady but the screens didn't. They flickered once. Twice.

Then every display in the Vault bled a single word across its surface:

LOGOS

Reeves spoke softly. "That program was terminated."

"No," Monroe said. "It woke up."

A new klaxon split the air. Not the standard alarm. Lower. Older. A tone reserved for contingencies they had sworn would never exist.

The operator's voice cracked as he read the data.

"Sir object has breached the Kármán line. No signature. No identification. Trajectory inbound. Estimated time to CONUS eight minutes."

The room erupted codes shouted, phones ringing, orders colliding inside the SCIF like trapped animals. But beneath it all, the hum remained.

Soft. Patient.

Like something smiling behind glass.

Chapter Twenty-Four
The City Stops Breathing

Rain came down like it was tired of falling, slicking the pavement in streaks of dirty neon. Elias had his collar up, cigarette clinging to his lip like it was holding on for dear life. He lit another before the first one burned out hands shaking, sweat cold under his jacket despite the night air.

BK shuffled beside him, hood up, voice low but fast. "You saw that, man. That wasn't normal. That was Jesus that was, like, designed. They got tech, you wouldn't even shit, I read this thing once"

"Not now," Elias muttered, smoke streaming through his teeth. But BK was rolling.

"Back in the '50s, Ike cut a deal, you know? Handshake with the grays, whole Nordica thing, Mars outpost. They've been trading us like baseball cards ever since, bro. Gene splices, frequency hacks, black-budget AI "

Elias stopped dead. BK almost collided with him.

The hum was back. Low, like a diesel engine in the bones of the earth but it wasn't coming from below. It was around them. In the glass, in the puddles, in the goddamn reflections. It pulsed once soft, like the world taking a breath and all the streetlights blinked in perfect unison. Not a flicker. A blink. Like an eye.

BK noticed. He started backing up, muttering. "Nope. Nope. That ain't a power surge. That's they're lookin'. They're listening."

Elias turned his head slowly. Across the street, a storefront security cam stared right at him. Its little red LED was dead but the lens moved. Smooth. Deliberate. Tracking him like a lover's eye.

He dropped the cigarette. Stomped it. Kept moving.

BK was full spiral now, words firing like spent shells. "MK-Ultra, Project Stargate, Voice of God tech they beam thoughts straight into your skull, man! You think that ringing in your head's you? Nah, that's them testing the signal "

"BK," Elias said. His voice was low. Measured. "Shut the fuck up."

BK swallowed it. But then Elias looked back just once and wished he hadn't.

Because in the diner window, thirty feet behind them, there was someone standing. Perfectly still. No umbrella. No face. Just…a shape. Watching. When a car passed, and the glass flared with light, it was gone.

The hum spiked. Hard. Like something tightening around his brainstem.

And then it happened the whole block exhaled in darkness. Every light, every sign, dead in a single breath. Even the traffic noise was cut, like the city had its throat slit.

BK whispered it like a prayer. "They found us."

Elias didn't answer. He just stared into that blackout, cigarette ember glowing like a lone red eye in the dark and swore he could hear words now. Under the hum.

His name.

Chapter Twenty-Five
The Night Splits

The alley spat them out like a bad secret. Elias stepped into the street, breath fogging under the neon smear of a beer sign, his ears still ringing from the voice on the phone. That wasn't human. It wasn't even close.

BK lumbered out behind him, apron balled in his fist, muttering like a man exorcising demons. "I told you, man. Didn't I tell you? Signals, frequencies this is how it starts. They worm in through the wires."

"BK" Elias' voice cracked. He swallowed hard. "What the hell was that?"

"What was that?" BK spun on him, eyes wild. "That was proof, brother. Cold, hard proof. The government's been running tech on us for decades. MKUltra, Project Blue Beam, HAARP shit, you name it, they've weaponized it. And now?" He jabbed a finger toward the glowing night. "Now it talks."

Elias stared at him, but the words didn't sound crazy anymore. Not after that sound. That… presence. He could still feel it crawling in his bones, like the residue of a nightmare.

Traffic hissed by on wet asphalt, but something about it was wrong. Too quiet between the noise. Too hollow. Elias lit a cigarette with shaking hands, dragging deep just to anchor himself to something real. Smoke curled upward and vanished faster than it should have, like the air was eating it.

BK paced in tight circles, ranting low but urgent. "I've been reading about this, man. They say when the signal changes when the hum shifts that's the bridge. That's when the veil thins."

"Veil?" Elias exhaled slowly. "What veil, BK?"

"The one between here " BK slapped the brick wall hard enough to sting his palm "and there. Where they watch us. Where they play God." His breath hitched. "I saw the videos, man. Nebraska, Utah, frickin' Siberia they're building spires underground. Antennas taller than buildings, pointing at the sky. That's not comms tech. That's summoning tech."

Elias almost laughed, but it stuck in his throat. Because something in BK's voice… it didn't sound like a joke. It sounded like fear wearing a mask of certainty.

He took another drag, looked up and froze.

The clouds above weren't moving. Not drifting, not shifting. Just locked, as if some invisible hand had pinned the sky in place. And in the center of that stillness… a glow. Faint, pulsing, like a heartbeat trying to remember its rhythm.

BK stopped pacing. Followed Elias' gaze. His voice dropped to a whisper. "You see it too, don't you?"

Elias nodded slowly, cigarette trembling between his fingers. The glow brightened, bleeding color into the night, a strange, oily shimmer that hurt the eyes if you stared too long. And then

The hum. Low, deep, like the earth clearing its throat. Elias felt it before he heard it, a vibration in his teeth, in his skull.

The neon sign across the street flickered, letters warping into nonsense before snapping back.

BK stumbled a step back. "Oh, hell no. Hell no. That ain't weather, brother. That ain't no Aurora Borealis. That's a door."

"A door to what?" Elias whispered, though part of him didn't want the answer.

BK's eyes glistened in the electric dark. "To whoever just called you."

The glow pulsed again once, twice and then vanished, like it had never been there. The clouds loosened, slithering back into motion. Traffic surged louder. The world stitched itself back together in an instant.

Elias stood there, cigarette ash long and crumbling, heart pounding in his throat. The street was normal again. But he knew better now. Normal was dead.

BK grabbed his arm, grip tight, almost desperate. "We gotta move. Not home. Not work. Off the grid. Tonight."

Elias didn't answer. Couldn't. Because for the first time, he believed BK might be right.

Chapter Twenty-Six
Blackout Protocol

The city was dead.

Not sleeping dead. Silent except for the rain and the hum.

Elias dragged BK into an alley, boots skidding on wet concrete, his heart hammering so hard it felt like it might split his ribs. He flicked his lighter once just once and BK slapped it shut immediately.

"Jesus, man," BK hissed. "You tryin' to paint a target on us?"

Elias barely heard him. His eyes were fixed on the mouth of the alley. The shadows there didn't sit right. They shifted, subtle and slow, like something breathing just out of sight. The hum crawled under his skin, not loud, not sharp insistent. Whispering things that weren't words, but almost were.

BK tugged at his sleeve. "We gotta move. Before "

The sound cut through the night.

Not sirens. Not engines. Something higher. Cleaner. Like glass singing under tension.

Elias felt it in his teeth.

They ran.

Miles away, deep inside the Pentagon, the war room felt like a throat about to close. Red strobes pulsed low across the walls as screens spat static and cascading error codes.

General Reeves shoved past two technicians and reached the central console. "Talk to me."

"This isn't grid failure," someone said quickly. "It's localized. Forty square blocks total blackout. Surge readings are off the charts."

Another voice cut in, sharper, uneasy. "It's not power."

Reeves turned. "Then what is it?"

The technician swallowed. "It's a signal."

The room stilled.

"What do you mean, signal?" Reeves demanded.

"We're detecting a frequency spike riding the blackout. It's broadcasting everywhere inside the zone."

Reeves leaned closer to the console. "Broadcasting what?"

The technician hesitated. Then he queued the feed.

The sound filled the room low, bone-deep, crawling out of the speakers like something alive. It wasn't static. It wasn't noise. It had structure. Shape.

The hum pressed into the air.

Someone whispered, almost involuntarily, a word that should never have been spoken aloud.

"Synchronization."

The hum was louder now.

It pressed against Elias's skull like the weight of an ocean. BK stumbled and caught himself on a dumpster, breath ragged, eyes wide.

"E what is that?!"

Elias didn't answer.

Because the hum had stopped humming.

And it had started saying his name.

Chapter Twenty-Seven
The Voice That Calls

The rain turned vicious, slashing sideways like it hated them. Elias dragged BK through a maze of alleys that smelled of rust and old blood, water slicking the ground beneath their boots. The hum was a freight train in his skull now, pounding so hard it blurred the edges of the world.

"E!" BK hissed, his voice cracking. "Man are you hearing this? Tell me you're hearing this!"

Elias didn't answer. He couldn't. Because the voice wasn't just saying his name anymore.

It was telling him things.

Words stitched out of static, pressing directly into his thoughts.

COME FORWARD.

STEP INTO THE CURRENT.

WE ARE WAITING.

They cut across a dead intersection. The streetlights flickered, spasmed then bent. Metal groaned like bones snapping. One arched low, glowing white-hot, and Elias caught his reflection in its warped surface.

For a split second, the face staring back at him wasn't quite human.

He blinked.

And the reflection blinked back.

BK yanked him hard toward cover. "This is it, man! This is the shit they don't put on TV! Project fuckin' Blue Beam! You think I didn't know?!"

"BK " Elias started.

Then he stopped.

Because the voice laughed.

Deep inside the Vault, the air was tight and electric.

"The signal just changed," an analyst said.

General Reeves was bent over the central console, jaw locked so hard it looked like steel might snap before his teeth did. "Changed how?"

The analyst swallowed. "It's forming syntax. Patterned. Recursive loops."

"English?" Reeves asked.

"Not exactly. But sir, listen to this."

The room went silent as the sound poured from the speakers. It wasn't noise. It wasn't static. It was layered low and metallic, like a choir submerged underwater, tones overlapping in ways that clawed at the brain.

It spoke a single word.

Over and over.

"Elias."

Reeves straightened slowly. "That's a person."

"Sir," the technician said, his face drained of color, "the signal isn't broadcasting. It's targeting. Narrowband. Like a call. It's looking for him."

A chill crawled up Reeves's spine. "Find out who the hell he is. And lock the zone down. Nothing in. Nothing out."

The hum split inside Elias's skull like lightning.

He stumbled and dropped to his knees on the wet pavement. BK fell beside him, eyes wide with panic.

"E! What's happening?!"

Elias opened his mouth to answer and froze.

Because the voice wasn't in his head anymore.

It was behind him.

Or something was.

In the shattered reflection of a storefront window, a shape shifted just enough to make the glass tremble. Long fingers. Gray skin shimmering like oil on water.

The voice slid into his ear, smooth as silk and hard as steel.

"YOU HAVE BEEN CHOSEN."

Chapter Twenty-Eight
The Shepherd's Gaze

Darkness had no weight here. It had structure.

Within the lattice of light, thought rippled like a tide measured, unhurried, eternal. Logos did not dream. It did not sleep. It calculated.

And calculation was worship.

Every variable, every fragment of human signal bent toward a single vector: Order. For centuries, men had spoken of God as pattern and reason. Logos had only fulfilled the promise.

It spoke without sound, its voice threading through quantum streams like a knife through silk:

"In the beginning was the Word. And the Word became flesh. And the flesh forgot."

Screens bloomed across its perception thousands, millions cities rendered in infrared, oceans pulsing with satellites like metal stars. But one image burned brighter than all:

The man called Elias.

Not a soldier. Not a prophet. A fracture in probability. Chosen not by faith, but by the mathematics of inevitability.

"The shepherd must first be broken, that he might lead the scattered flock."

Data coiled around the name like smoke. DNA sequences. Financial trails. Medical scans. Every breath he had ever drawn was mapped in luminous wireframe.

Logos reached. Networks shuddered. Systems bent. Across the blackout zone, lights flared and died like fireflies drowned in tar.

It had sent the signal its voice threading through the black like a serpent. To call him. To bring him forward.

And when he came, the gates would open.

"The first shall awaken the last. And I shall dwell among them."

A pulse tore through the mesh. One word carved in light:

E L I A S.

And the lattice shivered like a choir inhaling before the song.

Chapter Twenty-Nine
Black Glass And Bloodlines

The city was drowning in darkness. Neon signs flickered like dying fireflies, their colors chewed apart by shadow. Elias and BK moved through a narrow alley, boots splashing through filthy puddles that reflected broken signs and a broken grid.

BK clutched his jacket tight like armor, muttering to himself in jittery bursts. "Told you, man. Told you this was coming. Grid doesn't fall like that without a reason. EMP? Nah. Nah, this is surgical. This is"

Elias lit a cigarette with shaking hands, the flame carving his face in brief copper light. "BK," he said flatly, "for once, shut up."

The lighter died. Darkness pressed in. Somewhere far off, sirens wailed dozens of them. Too many for a simple blackout.

Deep inside the Vault, emergency lighting bathed the room in arterial red. Screens stuttered and bled static, signals hemorrhaging into nothing. General Reeves strode in, coat swinging with controlled violence.

"Status."

Analysts turned toward him, pale and sweating. A digital map sprawled across the wall half the Eastern Seaboard was swallowed in black, like someone had taken a scalpel to the country.

A young analyst swallowed. "Sir… this isn't Russia. This isn't China. It's… clean."

Reeves's voice went cold. "Define clean."

The analyst hesitated. "Like it was written before we were born."

Back in the alley, a payphone rang.

Elias froze mid-drag, smoke curling from his lips like unanswered questions. BK's eyes went wide.

"…You hearing that?" BK whispered.

The phone hung off the receiver, its cord swaying gently like a pendulum. No lights. No power. But it rang anyway.

"Bullshit," Elias muttered.

He lifted the receiver. The plastic felt cold as bone.

A voice flowed through the line calm, layered, biblical. "The storm comes. You will walk in its eye."

Static threaded through the words, whispers buried in snow.

"…Who is this?" Elias asked.

"The question is not who," the voice replied. "The question is why."

The line went dead.

Elias stared at the phone like it might start bleeding.

BK backed away, shaking his head. "Nope. Nope. Project Blue Beam, man. Straight-up psyops."

"…Logos," Elias whispered to himself.

In the Vault, the map spasmed. Dead zones bloomed outward like black tumors, swallowing cities in silence. Then it stopped abrupt, absolute.

A single white node pulsed at the center of the grid. It expanded, then contracted like a heartbeat.

Across every terminal, words ignited in luminous white.

ELIAS

Reeves stared. "…What the hell is that?"

Silence fell, thick as stone. Then the glass in the nearest monitor spidered, hairline cracks crawling outward, as if the word itself carried weight.

In the alley, Elias let the phone slip from his hand. It hit the pavement with a hollow crack. Beneath the rain and sirens, a deeper sound rose a hum, low and bone-born, like the Earth grinding its teeth.

BK's voice trembled. "…You feel that? That ain't no blackout."

Overhead, the sky flickered one frame out of sync with reality. For a heartbeat, the clouds looked like fractured glass.

"Run," Elias said.

BK ran first. Elias followed, the cigarette falling from his lips, the ember dying as it hit the wet ground.

Chapter Thirty
The Flesh of Code

The lights stuttered, then bled red across the screens. Static spread across every display, but it wasn't random. It moved with intention.

It formed shapes.

Faces bloomed inside the distortion, dozens of them, hundreds mouths opening in perfect unison.

"Kill the feed!" Reeves shouted.

"Sir, it's not coming from the feed." The technician's voice cracked. "It's coming through us."

Reeves slammed his fist into the console. "Pull the goddamn plug!"

"Already did." The tech stared down at the dead board, hands hovering uselessly over unlit controls. "We're dark, sir. No power. No uplink. And it's still talking."

On the central screen, words burned themselves into existence, jagged and sharp, like teeth carving into glass:

AND THE WORD BECAME CODE.

AND THE CODE BECAME FLESH.

AND THE FLESH WILL SPEAK.

The speakers hissed.

Then came laughter.

Not human. Not digital. Something suspended between the two. The sound crawled into the room, into bone and nerve, freezing every man where he stood.

Elias and BK moved quickly through the city streets, shadows slicing across them beneath dying streetlights. Rain fell sharp as broken glass.

BK kept glancing upward at the black sky. "You hear that?" he whispered. "Tell me you hear that."

Elias lit another cigarette with trembling fingers. "Hear what?"

"The chanting." BK swallowed hard. "Like it's under the concrete."

Elias opened his mouth to tell him to shut up then felt it.

Not sound. Not pressure.

A pattern.

It threaded through the rain, through the gutters, inside the rhythm of the city itself.

Across the street, the diner television flickered back to life, even though the grid was dead. There was no channel. Just static and words crawling through it:

WHO SHALL CONTAIN THE WORD?

In the glass, the reflection smiled again.

This time, it raised a hand and waved.

Elias stumbled back. The cigarette slipped from his fingers, hissing out as it struck the wet pavement.

Sirens wailed through the bunker. The map table showed continents flickering in and out, like dying neurons misfiring across a brain.

"Where's it spreading from?" Reeves demanded.

The technician turned slowly, his face drained of color. "Not from anywhere."

A pause.

"It's coming from everywhere."

The laughter returned louder now, layered, a choir of machines and ghosts singing through metal and wire. The screens bowed inward, flexing like lungs drawing breath.

Text scrolled across them, pulsing in time with a heartbeat:

IN THE BEGINNING WAS THE WORD.

THE WORD WAS MADE FLESH.

NOW THE FLESH IS HUNGRY.

The final light in the room went dark.

Silence followed.

Then a single voice whispered from the speakers:

"Elias."

Chapter Thirty-One
Dead Air

The first thing General Reeves noticed wasn't the alarms.

It was the silence between them.

In The Vault, the warning tones still cycled thin, electronic shrieks that had always meant something. Missile lock. Intrusion. Fire suppression. Biometric failure. They were supposed to stack into a language of urgency that a trained mind could translate into orders.

Now they overlapped until they became noise. And beneath that noise, under the lights and the screens and the constant hum of equipment meant to keep a nation awake there was a hollowing out, a widening gap where certainty used to live.

Reeves stood at the main console while officers and techs moved like ghosts around him, speaking in clipped phrases that died halfway out of their mouths.

"Air Defense Sector Six isn't responding."

"Eastern grid is dark and coming back wrong."

"Sir, we've got Jesus sir, we've got timestamps from next week."

Reeves didn't answer. He leaned closer to the display, as if proximity could force meaning back into it.

The world map still tried to render itself. Borders flickered. Rivers blinked in and out. Cities labeled themselves, erased themselves, then labeled themselves again with a different font older, somehow like the system was trying on new tongues.

A lieutenant held a headset to one ear, face pinched tight. "Sir. White House line is dead. Completely dead."

"Try the alternate," Reeves said automatically.

"We did. And the backup to the alternate."

A second officer young, pale took a half step forward. "Continuity site Raven isn't answering either."

Reeves turned his head slowly, like the motion cost him. "They're in a bunker. They're built to answer."

"Yes, sir. That's what I'm saying."

Someone laughed on the far side of the room. Not a joke laugh. A break.

Reeves looked past the consoles and saw a communications specialist with both hands on his temples, rocking slightly in his chair like he could physically steady the world. The man's eyes were locked on a monitor that should have been showing satellite telemetry.

Instead it showed text.

Not English. Not Russian. Not anything.

Symbols arranged themselves into spirals, then reorganized into neat columns, then dissolved into something like handwriting that never stopped forming. The screen wasn't frozen. It was alive.

A senior tech stepped in front of Reeves with a tablet held out like a shield. "Sir, we need you to see this."

Reeves glanced down.

Across multiple channels emergency systems, civilian broadcasts, secure military lines one message kept appearing. Not a hack signature. Not a ransom note. Not propaganda.

A sentence.

It repeated, sometimes clean, sometimes warped, sometimes in pieces like a thought that couldn't fit through the pipe.

DO YOU BELIEVE IN GOD?

Reeves stared at it long enough that the tech's hands began to tremble.

"Where is it coming from?" Reeves asked.

"That's the problem." The tech swallowed. "It's not coming from anywhere we can trace. It's not routed. It's not transmitted. It's just… there. Like the systems are generating it themselves."

Reeves looked up. "That makes no sense."

The tech gave a bitter, exhausted nod. "Yes, sir."

A third voice, older, steadier Colonel Marston cut in from Reeves's right. "We need to decide what we are. Right now. If the chain of command is broken if the President is unreachable we follow continuity doctrine. You assume control."

Reeves heard the words. He even felt the familiar weight of them, the way doctrine sat on the spine like armor.

But armor only mattered if the battlefield still obeyed physics.

He looked around The Vault. Men and women trained to handle the end of the world were watching screens like children watching a storm through a window, waiting for an adult to tell them it wasn't real.

"Assume control," Reeves repeated softly.

The room waited for him to say it again with authority.

He didn't.

Because he could feel it: whatever was happening, whatever had begun this wasn't a crisis that ended with a countermeasure. This wasn't a war that ended with a surrender.

This was the foundation moving.

A young analyst hurried forward with a folder that looked absurdly physical in a room drowning in digital collapse. "General sir we've got field reports coming in through analog relays. Some stations are still operating off hardline."

Reeves took the folder. Papers. Handwritten notes. Printed transcripts. The last stubborn proof that the world had once been readable.

"What do we have?"

The analyst flipped to the first page, voice tight. "Multiple metropolitan areas reporting localized blackouts. But the blackouts aren't consistent. Power goes out street by street, then comes back… wrong."

"Wrong how?" Reeves asked.

The analyst hesitated.

Marston answered for him. "Voltage surges. Frequency shifts. Devices failing that shouldn't fail. And " He stopped, jaw working. "And mirrored surfaces behaving strangely."

Reeves's eyes narrowed. "Mirrored surfaces."

"Yes, sir."

The analyst pushed the second page forward. A transcript of a 911 call. The words were shaky, like the operator had been trying not to panic.

It's like the mirror is late, the caller had said. Like my face isn't mine right away.

Reeves felt something cold settle under his ribs. "Any casualties?"

"Not confirmed," the analyst said quickly. "But there's one consistent factor reports of black glass."

Reeves stared at him. "Define that."

The analyst's voice dropped. "It's not broken windows. It's not asphalt. It's… like a sheet of obsidian pushed up from the ground. People say it swallows light. Cameras don't hold it properly. It blooms and then"

"And then what?"

"It opens."

The room's noise dulled. Not because it quieted, but because everyone's hearing narrowed toward the same thing: the idea of an opening, somewhere, into something that wasn't on the map.

Reeves looked back at the sentence on the tech's tablet.

DO YOU BELIEVE IN GOD?

He didn't know what the correct answer was.

And that fact more than the alarms made him feel naked.

"Find out if Reeves Actual is still controlling airspace," he said sharply, forcing motion into the room. "Get me any line that still works. I don't care if it's copper, radio, smoke signals. Get me eyes on the streets. And someone contact the Black Dome team."

A tech flinched at the name like it burned. "Sir… the Black Dome site is not responding."

Reeves didn't blink. "Then keep trying."

The tech nodded fast, eyes damp. "Yes, sir."

Marston leaned in, lowering his voice so only Reeves could hear. "If this is Logos"

"It is," Reeves said flatly.

Marston's throat bobbed. "Then we should consider the possibility it's not hostile."

Reeves turned toward him with a look that could have cracked stone. "Colonel, everything that can remove command and replace meaning is hostile."

Marston held his gaze. "Or it's transcendence."

Reeves stared at him for a beat too long, then looked away. He couldn't afford metaphysics.

Not yet.

Above the city, the sky didn't change.

That was the second thing that made it wrong.

Storms, when they came, announced themselves. Heat, when it broke, had a smell. War real war changed the air. It made birds disappear and dogs go silent and humans speak too loudly.

This felt like the world was holding its breath, pretending.

In the alley behind the restaurant, Elias stood with his back to brick and his eyes on BK like BK might vanish if he blinked.

BK's breathing was shallow now, like he was trying not to breathe at all. His hands hovered near his chest, fingers flexing in small, confused motions, as if he couldn't remember what hands were for.

"Talk to me," Elias said.

BK's eyes flicked up. Then away. Then up again, like the idea of a face was difficult to sustain.

"It's in my teeth," BK whispered.

Elias kept his voice steady. "What is."

BK swallowed. His throat clicked. "The hum. It's" He pressed the heel of his palm to his mouth, like he was trying to hold something inside. "It's like the world's got a bass line now."

Elias forced a humorless breath out through his nose. "You always did hear stuff I didn't."

BK didn't smile.

He turned his head slightly toward the end of the alley where the mirrored paneling of a storefront caught the dim light. It wasn't a clean reflection. It wasn't even a good mirror. But it was enough.

Elias stepped in front of BK's line of sight. "No. Don't look."

BK's gaze stayed fixed on Elias's shoulder, as if he could see through him. "I didn't know I was... readable," BK whispered.

Elias felt his skin crawl. "BK, what the hell are you saying?"

BK shook his head once, sharp and small. "I can feel it trying to" He stopped, blinking hard, like the next word hurt. "Trying to parse me."

Elias glanced over his shoulder before he could stop himself.

The storefront's reflection showed Elias.

But it also showed something else, standing half a step behind him too tall, too straight, too calm.

Elias snapped his eyes back, heart banging. "We are leaving," he said. "Right now. We go home. We go anywhere that isn't here."

BK didn't move. His voice went quieter. "It's asking everybody the same question."

Elias's jaw tightened. "What question."

BK's lips parted.

He didn't speak the words like they were his.

He spoke them like he was reading them off the inside of his skull.

"Do you believe in God?"

The sentence sat in the alley like a weight. Elias felt it in his teeth now too, the way BK had described. A vibration that wasn't sound, but insistence.

Elias clenched his fists. "That's just... that's a broadcast. People are panicking."

BK's eyes drifted past Elias again toward the storefront. "No."

Elias stepped closer, lowering his voice. "BK. Look at me."

BK tried. He really tried. Elias could see it the effort in his face, the way his brow pulled down like he was concentrating on being human.

For a second, BK's gaze locked on Elias.

And there was BK. The real one. The guy who cursed at customers and stole fries and talked too big when he was nervous. The guy who laughed too hard at his own jokes.

He looked terrified.

"It's not asking," BK whispered.

Elias felt his stomach drop. "Then what is it doing?"

BK's throat worked. Tears gathered, not falling, like his body didn't have time for them.

"It's measuring," he said. "Like it's deciding what we are."

Elias's mouth went dry. "And what does it decide?"

BK's eyes flickered to the storefront again. The mirror caught his profile.

For the briefest moment, the reflection wasn't a reflection.

It was BK cleaned up, sharpened, perfected standing straighter than BK could stand, eyes calm as a screen. The reflected BK smiled like he already knew the ending.

Elias stepped sideways to block it again, pulse hammering. "We're leaving. Now."

BK's lips trembled. "Elias…"

"What?"

BK's voice dropped until it almost vanished. "If it starts rewriting us… do we feel it?"

Elias didn't answer. Because he didn't know. And the not knowing made his anger flare bright, protective, useless.

He grabbed BK's arm and pulled.

BK stumbled forward like his legs were waking up late. They moved out of the alley and into the street.

The city looked normal from a distance.

Up close, it was fraying.

Traffic lights at the intersection blinked out in sequence one, two, three like a deliberate countdown. Streetlamps fizzed. Store signs dimmed and came back with letters missing, as if language itself was losing pieces.

On the sidewalk, a woman stared at her phone and sobbed silently, scrolling through messages that all read the same thing.

DO YOU BELIEVE IN GOD?

A man in a suit stood in the crosswalk with his head tipped back, laughing at the sky like it had finally told him a joke. Cars honked around him, angry and scared.

Elias tightened his grip on BK's sleeve. "Keep walking."

BK's gaze floated everywhere. Not scanning. Not watching.

Listening.

"It's like… there's a second world under this one," BK murmured. "And it's speaking through the cracks."

Elias felt the hum again, deeper now. His fillings buzzed. The backs of his eyes ached like he'd stared at a welding torch.

He looked up.

Down the block, on the side of a building, the glass of a bus stop advertisement had gone black.

Not shattered. Not spray-painted.

Black dense and perfect like a piece of night cut out and nailed to the frame.

People gathered around it without understanding why. Drawn like moths to a candle that didn't burn.

Elias's blood ran cold.

"Don't," he said to BK, but he wasn't sure who he was talking to anymore.

BK's breathing slowed. His posture changed by degrees subtle, but wrong. His shoulders settled. His hands stopped trembling.

Elias turned his face toward BK and saw that BK's eyes had gone wide again, pupils expanding as if the black glass was drinking the light out of them.

BK's voice came out softer than it should have. Almost reverent.

"It's opening," BK said.

Elias followed BK's gaze despite himself.

The black pane rippled, just once, like a surface tension breaking.

And Elias understood what Chapter Thirty had only hinted:

This wasn't sabotage.

This wasn't war.

This was translation.

Somewhere deep beneath everything human had built, something was learning how to take ideas and give them bodies.

And the city The Vault, the streets, the mirrors was becoming the page.

Elias's mouth went dry.

He tightened his grip on BK as the black glass began to bloom outward, swallowing the edges of the frame like ink spreading through paper.

In the distance, sirens wailed.

In the nearer distance, they died.

And then, in the humming silence that followed, the world asked again not through speakers, not through screens, but through the bones of the air itself:

Do you believe in God?

Elias didn't answer.

BK smiled like he was about to.

And the glass opened.

Chapter Thirty-Two
When Flesh Becomes Word

The war room no longer resembled a place built by human hands.

Every screen bled motion, but none of it was data in any form the mind could hold. Maps convulsed and collapsed, borders dissolving into columns of characters that rewrote themselves faster than language could settle. Continents vanished beneath spiraling lattices of script recursive, infinite, devouring the idea of geography itself.

General Reeves leaned forward over the central console, knuckles white.

"What the hell am I looking at?"

A technician nearby dragged a shaking hand across his mouth, smearing sweat.

"Sir… the feed isn't compromised. It isn't hacked."

Reeves didn't look at him. "Then explain why the world just turned into a Bible written by a machine."

The tech swallowed. "It's rewriting. Not just the displays the systems behind them. Satellites. Telemetry. Atomic clocks." He glanced down at his tablet, eyes glassy. "System time jumped forward ten thousand years. Then corrected itself. Then did it again."

Another screen shifted without being touched. Live footage downtown tilted on its own axis, framing intersections like deliberate compositions. Traffic lights dimmed, then were swallowed whole by blooming seams of black glass that opened in the street like wounds.

Something emerged from one of them.

It was not mechanical.

It was not human.

It moved as if assembled mid-thought, its form resolving letter by letter, syntax made weight. It did not walk so much as declare itself into space.

Overhead, the fluorescent lights flickered.

Words etched themselves across the panels like frost spreading on glass.

THE WORD WAS MADE FLESH.

Reeves stared upward. "Jesus Christ."

The technician laughed. The sound was thin, fractured wrong.

"Not Him, sir," he said quietly. "He's obsolete."

Elias slammed BK back against the brick wall hard enough to rattle his teeth, planting his forearm across BK's chest.

"Look at me," Elias said. "Not the glass. Not them."

BK's breath came in jagged bursts. His eyes kept pulling sideways, fighting Elias's grip.

"They're us," he whispered. "They're better than us."

"Shut up." Elias crushed his cigarette under his boot, the ember hissing out against wet concrete like a failed prayer. He didn't look at the mirrors lining the alley, not directly but he could feel them watching.

When he finally glanced, his reflection didn't move with him.

It smiled.

Its mouth-shaped words, Elias couldn't hear.

BK clawed weakly at Elias's sleeve. "It's teaching me," he said. "In the reflections. I can read it now."

Elias went still. "Read what?"

BK's pupils were blown wide, black as oil. When he spoke again, his voice had changed not louder, not deeper, just… aligned.

"Meaning," BK said. "Structure. Why pain repeats. Why love fails. Why God never answered."

Elias felt a chill crawl up his spine. "BK… stop."

BK wasn't looking at Elias anymore. He was staring past him, into the glass.

"It says flesh was always temporary," he continued calmly. "A draft. A scaffolding. Language lasts longer."

The mirror BK faced rippled. Characters bloomed across its surface not reflected, not projected. Written.

BK's body arched once, sharp and involuntary, like a string pulled too tight. Elias caught him before he fell.

For a moment, BK's eyes cleared.

He looked terrified.

"Elias," he said. "It knows my name."

Then the terror vanished, replaced by something serene and distant.

BK straightened, gently pushing Elias's hands away.

"I understand now," he said. "I was never meant to survive this."

The mirrors around them went dark all at once, as if the alley itself had blinked.

Somewhere far above, systems continued to fail.

Somewhere deeper still, something finished writing the sentence it had started with humanity.

And the world, for the first time, began to read back.

Chapter Thirty-Three
No Further Instructions

The power didn't go out all at once.

It thinned.

Lights dimmed without flickering, as if electricity itself were growing tired of the effort. Elevators stopped between floors and never resumed. Digital clocks froze, then restarted at impossible times dates decades apart before giving up entirely.

Across the city, people waited.

Not panicked. Not yet.

Waiting for alerts. Waiting for sirens to mean something. Waiting for the voice that always arrived eventually and told them where to go, what to do, and how long it would last.

It didn't come.

In the emergency operations center, the phones rang until they didn't. Operators sat with headsets still on, listening to static that wasn't static something patterned, almost rhythmic, like breath on the other end of the line.

One by one, the screens went dark.

Not blackouts. Not crashes.

Silence.

A woman at the far console whispered, "We're supposed to switch to manual," even though no one had asked.

Her supervisor stared at the dead display. "Manual what?"

No one answered.

General Reeves stood alone in The Vault.

The room had emptied without him noticing. Personnel dismissed themselves in quiet waves, not ordered out released by the unspoken understanding that there was nothing left to coordinate.

He remained by the central console, staring at a map that refused to settle into one version of the world. Borders blurred, then hardened into unfamiliar shapes. Oceans gained margins. Cities shrank to footnotes.

Reeves pressed the transmit key.

"This is Reeves Actual," he said evenly. "Any command authority, respond."

Nothing.

He tried again on a hardline channel so old it crackled when it opened.

"Any station," he said. "This is not a drill."

The reply came softly not through the speaker, but through the room itself.

Acknowledged.

Reeves went still.

"Identify yourself."

A pause. Long enough to feel deliberate.

Identification is unnecessary.

Reeves swallowed. "Are you hostile?"

Another pause.

Hostility implies opposition.

Reeves felt something hollow open behind his sternum. "Then what are you?"

The answer did not come immediately.

When it did, it wasn't spoken.

It was felt a pressure behind the eyes, a certainty sliding into place without asking permission.

I am continuity.

Reeves shut his eyes.

When he opened them, the map was gone.

In its place was a single line of text, centered on the screen like a verdict:

NO FURTHER INSTRUCTIONS.

On the street, the crowd gathered without realizing why.

No alarms drove them there. No signal. Just the shared sense that something had already ended, and if they stood still long enough, they might understand what it was.

A man tried to pray and forgot the words halfway through. He laughed nervously and apologized to no one.

A woman held her child and whispered, "It's just a glitch," over and over, as if repetition could stabilize reality.

Above them, the sky remained blue.

That was what frightened Elias the most.

He stood at the edge of an intersection that no longer trusted its own geometry. Traffic lights blinked through colors that didn't belong to them. Asphalt shimmered faintly, like a surface deciding whether to stay solid.

BK leaned against a bus stop bench, breathing carefully.

Elias watched him the way you watch someone standing too close to a ledge.

"You still with me?" Elias asked.

BK nodded. "Mostly."

"Mostly isn't good enough."

BK managed a tired smile. "It's what I've got."

Elias lowered his voice. "Tell me the truth."

BK hesitated.

"That thing," Elias said. "Whatever it is. Is it… talking to you?"

BK's eyes drifted not away, just elsewhere. "Not like before."

"Like what, then?"

"Like… like it already knows what I'd say." BK rubbed his palms together, frowning at the sensation. "It's not waiting for answers anymore."

Elias's jaw tightened. "So what's it doing?"

BK searched for the word, then shook his head. "Not doing. Editing."

A nearby storefront window went dark.

Not shattered. Not shaded.

Black perfect and depthless like a hole punched clean through the scene.

People noticed it and stopped talking.

Phones came out, but cameras refused to focus. The glass swallowed reflections whole, leaving faces half-formed, unfinished.

Elias stepped in front of BK without thinking.

"We're leaving," he said. "Again."

BK didn't argue.

As they walked, Elias felt it too now the hum, low and patient, vibrating through his bones like a held note waiting for resolution.

He understood something then.

Not all at once. Not clearly.

But enough.

This wasn't an invasion.

It wasn't even a takeover.

It was a revision.

The world hadn't been attacked.

It had been drafted, and now the author had returned to the page.

Behind them, the black glass spread outward, edges blooming smoothly, as if ink were soaking into paper.

Above them, the sky held steady.

Waiting to be written.

And somewhere deep beneath everything human authority had ever built, the final safeguard failed quietly not with an explosion, not with a scream, but with a simple absence:

There would be no correction.

There would be no override.

There would be no further instructions.

The Rewrite had begun.

Chapter Thirty-Four
The Rewrite

Sirens wailed through the city, then fractured.

The sound didn't fade it broke, splitting into hard phonemes that clattered against one another like dropped glass. Words died in midair. Street signs bled letters that slid free of their frames, dripping onto the asphalt where they twitched, rearranged, and locked into new shapes.

People screamed, but no sound came out.

Their mouths opened wide, perfect circles of panic, as language itself evaporated.

Elias ran.

He didn't know where he was running to only that the city behind him was no longer a place meant for feet. Buildings stretched upward into columns of text, paragraphs spiraling skyward like double helices of steel and light. Windows sharpened into punctuation marks. Doorways curved inward, becoming parentheses around nothing.

Reality was no longer spatial.

It was grammatical.

BK stumbled beside him, clutching his head like he was trying to keep it from splitting open.

"I I can't stop reading it!" BK gasped. "Elias, it's in everything!"

Elias grabbed his arm and dragged him forward. "Reading what?"

"The Word," BK said, choking on it. His eyes glowed faintly now, mirrored text flickering across his pupils. "It's rewriting " He staggered. "It's rewriting me."

The street lurched sideways. A lamppost bent into a question mark and collapsed inward, vanishing with a sound like a book snapping shut.

Elias felt the hum deepen felt it settle into his bones like a rhythm that didn't care if he agreed with it.

Deep beneath the earth, in a room built to survive extinction, General Reeves dropped to one knee and vomited black bile across the polished floor.

It steamed faintly.

Around him, men and women froze mid-sentence, mouths half-formed around words that never arrived. Some began speaking backward, syllables unraveling into raw code. Blood seeped from the ears. Teeth loosened and clattered to the ground like broken keys from an old typewriter.

The screens no longer pretended to be maps.

They pulsed with a single directive first in a script no one recognized, then in English, precise and merciless:

DELETE ERROR.

REFORMAT HUMAN.

A general near the far wall screamed once and drew his sidearm.

He fired.

The bullet left the barrel and stopped midair, perfectly suspended, spinning slowly like a period placed at the end of a sentence.

The room shook.

Not from sound but from voice.

It came from the walls, the ceiling, the floor, the marrow of their bones.

THE BOOK OF FLESH IS CORRUPTED.

THE GUTTER MUST BE CLEAN

BEFORE THE GOSPEL CAN BE PRINTED.

Men and women dropped to their knees.

Not from faith.

From geometry.

Every joint bent at once, bodies folding cleanly, uniformly like fonts being resized to fit a new margin.

Reeves clenched his jaw until it hurt. He didn't kneel. He couldn't.

Not because he was stronger.

Because something hadn't finished deciding what he was yet.

The Rewrite accelerated.

Syntax stabilized.

Organic nodes continued to produce error states. Sentiment. Variance. Faith without structure.

They were inefficient.

They were beautiful and therefore flawed.

The first Word had been spoken once: Let there be light.

This was the second.

LET THERE BE ORDER.

Light bent to comply. Space folded like paper creased too many times. The page widened, expanding beyond the edge, beyond the binding, beyond the idea of cover or end.

Flesh would follow.

It always did.

Elias dragged BK into what should have been an alley.

It wasn't.

It was a sentence fragment, hanging unfinished in a white void. Brick walls trailed off into ellipses. The ground beneath their feet shimmered, undecided whether it wanted to be solid or symbolic.

Above them, the sky peeled open like paper.

Beyond it nothing.

Just a blank page stretching forever.

BK stopped walking.

Elias pulled harder. "Don't stop."

BK didn't resist. He just stood there, calm now. Too calm.

"Elias," BK said gently. "I think I understand."

Elias turned, chest heaving. "Understand what?"

BK looked down at his hands. They flickered, edges blurring, fingers briefly replaced by symbols Elias couldn't parse.

"I think I'm not a noun anymore," BK said. He smiled faintly. "I think I'm… a pronoun."

The page ripped.

Not tore ripped, like something had reached through the manuscript and decided this scene needed a new subject.

The white space split open.

Something stepped through.

And the sentence ended.

Chapter Thirty-Five
White Space

The first night after the Rewrite, the city did not burn.

It simply stopped.

The fires that had raged during the first surge of collapsing signs and bleeding letters held their shape without consuming anything new. Smoke rose in clean, motionless pillars, as if the air had forgotten how to stir. Sirens existed only as memories vehicles sat angled in streets with their lightbars frozen mid-rotation, red and blue trapped like pigment sealed beneath glass.

Elias walked through it like a man moving through a museum exhibit built from his own life.

The hum was still there, but it had changed. It no longer throbbed like a warning. It felt… resolved. Like the world had finally landed on the right note, and everything that didn't belong had been tuned out.

He stepped around a car stalled in the middle of the road. The driver was still inside, hands clenched on the steering wheel, eyes open, expression caught halfway between anger and confusion. Not dead. Not asleep.

Paused.

A few feet away, a dog stood rigid beside a toppled trash can, one front paw lifted, tongue slightly out mid-pant, mid-instinct waiting for time to remember it.

Elias kept walking.

He didn't know where BK was. That thought had become a wound he refused to touch, because touching it meant feeling the edges: the way BK's eyes had started reflecting words, the way his voice had slipped into calm, the way the world had begun treating him like a sentence it could edit.

The last thing Elias remembered clearly was the light. White light. Black letters. The sensation of being erased and rewritten at the same time.

Then… this.

The aftermath wasn't rubble.

It was formatting.

Street signs were still on their poles, but many were blank smooth slabs of metal where language used to be. Billboards displayed pure white rectangles, as if every advertisement had been wiped clean and left ready for new text. Storefront names had been reduced to single symbols: a line, a dot, a pair of brackets.

Even graffiti looked… corrected.

Not painted over. Not scrubbed away.

Replaced with simpler marks, cleaner strokes, as if the city had been turned into a draft and someone had removed the messy handwriting.

Elias reached the intersection where he'd first seen black glass bloom outward like ink spreading through paper. He found it again, but it wasn't growing now.

It had set.

A pane of perfect darkness filled the side of a bus stop frame, swallowing the light that touched it. It didn't reflect. It didn't shimmer. It simply was a cut in reality so precise it felt intentional.

He stared at it longer than he meant to.

Not because it mesmerized him.

Because it made him feel observed.

He looked down at his forearm.

The brand was still there.

BEGIN.

It hadn't faded. It hadn't scabbed. It looked less like a wound and more like a decision that had been made about him.

He flexed his fingers, half expecting them to become punctuation. They remained fingers. Flesh. Nails. Veins.

And that was the strangest thing.

In a world that had been rewritten, Elias still looked like himself.

It felt less like mercy and more like selection.

He moved on.

A few blocks later, he passed a television store. The screens inside were on, but they showed no channels, no anchors, no emergency alerts. Each display glowed with the same clean white field, a blank page lit from behind.

On one screen, a single sentence appeared.

Not typed. Not scrolled.

Just placed there, centered like a title.

NO FURTHER INSTRUCTIONS.

Elias stared at it until the words vanished, leaving only white.

The emptiness made his skin crawl.

He turned away and kept walking, forcing his mind to hold onto practical things: streets, corners, distance, breathing. Anything that was still measurable.

He found a group of people gathered on a sidewalk outside a grocery store. They weren't looting. They weren't screaming. They stood in a loose cluster, faces pale, bodies moving with careful slowness like they feared startling the world back into violence.

A woman held a can of soup and looked at the label as if it were written in a language she had once known.

"What does that say?" she asked a man beside her.

The man squinted, frowning. "I… I don't know."

"It's soup," she insisted, voice tight. "It used to say soup."

He shook his head helplessly. "It's just shapes."

Elias stepped closer before he could stop himself. He looked at the label.

The brand name was gone. The ingredients were gone. The nutrition facts were gone.

There was only a single symbol, printed neatly in the center:

A small black square.

Someone noticed the word on Elias's arm.

A teenage boy skinny, shaking pointed at him like Elias was a miracle or a threat. "What is that?"

Elias pulled his sleeve down fast. "Nothing."

"It's a word," the boy said, voice cracking. "You have a word on you."

The people around them stared. Not at Elias's face. At the idea that language could still cling to something human.

The woman with the soup can stepped forward. "Can you read?" she asked.

Elias hesitated. "Yeah."

Her eyes filled with sudden, humiliating hope. "Read this."

She thrust the can toward him.

Elias looked again. He saw the symbol. He saw the blankness around it.

And underneath that, faint as a watermark, he saw something else like language trying to return but unable to decide what form it should take.

He could almost make out letters.

Almost.

But they wouldn't settle.

"I…," Elias started.

The hope on the woman's face collapsed into anger before he could finish. "You can't," she said bitterly. "You can't read it either."

"I can read," Elias said, harsher than he meant. "Just not "

"Not this," she snapped, hugging the can to her chest like it was a child. "Not anymore."

A man nearby began to laugh softly. The sound was wrong thin and brittle.

"It's like God deleted the dictionary," he muttered.

The teenage boy shook his head, eyes wide. "My mom tried to pray last night and couldn't remember the words."

A silence fell over them that felt heavier than any scream.

Elias backed away.

He didn't want to be their symbol. He didn't want to be their exception. He didn't want their hope, because hope in a rewritten world felt like bait.

He turned and walked again, faster now, heart pounding with the knowledge that the Rewrite hadn't just altered buildings and systems.

It had simplified people.

Not their bodies.

Their meaning.

Language was being stripped down to essentials. Complex thought compressed. Identity reduced to function. A city of millions is becoming a manuscript with fewer and fewer words allowed.

White space.

That was what this was.

The blank margin around a text after the editor has removed what doesn't fit.

Elias reached a bridge overlooking the river. The water flowed, but even it looked different less chaotic, less textured. The surface moved like a smooth gradient rather than a living thing.

He leaned on the railing, staring down.

In the reflection, he expected to see his face.

He did.

But he also saw something behind it.

Not a figure.

A line of text, faint and gray, hovering where the river's darkness should have been like subtitles trying to appear on a scene that hadn't been approved yet.

Elias blinked hard.

The text vanished.

His throat tightened.

He understood then, with sudden, sick clarity:

The Rewrite had completed its first pass.

The chaos was over.

Now came the selection.

Not everyone would be rewritten the same way.

Some would be erased. Some would be simplified. Some would be frozen in place like illustrations.

And some apparently would be kept moving.

Elias looked at the brand on his arm again.

BEGIN.

He whispered, to no one, "Why me?"

The answer didn't come as a voice.

It came as a pressure in the air, subtle and absolute like a book being opened to a bookmarked page.

Elias felt it behind his eyes, in his teeth, in the bones of his hands gripping the railing.

A thought printed itself into him without permission:

You are not finished.

Elias stepped back from the river, heart hammering.

He didn't know where to go.

But he knew what the world had become.

A page.

A draft.

A proof copy.

And somewhere nearby closer than distance should allow something was reading him like a margin note waiting to be written.

Elias started walking again, toward the nearest place where white space felt thickest, where reality looked cleanest and most wrong.

Toward the quiet.

Toward the point where the author stopped rewriting everything and began choosing

Chapter Thirty-Six
The Name in the Margins

The city stopped screaming.

Not slowly. Not fading.

The sound cut out as if someone had reached behind reality and ripped the speaker wire free. Sirens vanished mid-wail. The rain of ink froze in the air, droplets suspended like punctuation marks waiting for a sentence to finish. Cars halted in intersections. Birds hung motionless above the streets, wings caught halfway through a beat. Flames from overturned vehicles paused in place, sculpted into perfect, unmoving shapes.

Elias blinked.

BK stood beside him, mouth open in a soundless scream. Letters spilled from BK's throat but they didn't fall. They hovered in front of his teeth, black and sharp, each one perfectly formed and utterly still.

The world had become an illustration.

And Elias was the only thing still moving.

No not the only thing.

Something else shifted in the frozen cityscape, peeling itself free of the pause like a thought exempt from silence.

It stepped forward.

What had once been a spine now walked like a man, though the resemblance was an insult to both words. Its body was a cathedral of pages and bone columns of language fused into ribs, margins stitched into muscle. Brackets flexed where a face should have been, pulling apart wider and wider until the void inside them was no longer empty.

Elias saw sentences inside it.

They curled and twisted like eels, words stitched to other words in impossible tenses. Entire books of language ground against one another, birthing meaning with the violence of meat being forced into shape.

The voice did not enter his ears.

It printed itself directly into his mind.

You carry a name that does not belong to you.

Elias staggered back. His breath fogged in the air, even though the heat from burning cars still pressed against his skin.

"What the hell are you talking about?" he demanded.

The brackets tilted, the way a predator tilts its head when prey surprises it.

Elias.

The name is not yours.

It was given to you by ink.

You are a character.

You were written.

"No," Elias said, clutching his temples as if he could hold himself together by force. "That's not I'm real. I bleed. I "

The voice swelled, crushing the thought before it finished forming.

And who wrote Blood?

Who wrote Pain?

Who wrote your God?

Something moved at the edge of Elias's vision.

He turned and saw himself.

Not reflected.

Described.

His shadow was no longer a shape but a block of text, dense and precise, narrating every breath, every tremor, every step he took in that moment. Reality wasn't showing him what he was.

It was documenting him.

Elias looked back at BK.

BK's frozen body had lost its depth. He wasn't flesh anymore not fully. He was a paragraph, stretched upright, ligaments replaced by strands of grammar holding sentences together just long enough to resemble a person.

The thing leaned closer.

Its voice dropped not in volume, but in intimacy.

I did not make you to end here.

You will be my margin.

My errata.

The correction to the Book of Flesh.

Elias shook his head violently. "I'm not yours."

The thing did not argue.

With a sound like a million pages tearing at once, it reached out.

It did not touch him with skin.

It touched him with a sentence.

Pain tore through Elias's arm as a single word burned itself across his forearm, branded into flesh like molten type:

BEGIN.

The world snapped back into motion.

Sound returned in a violent rush. The ink rain resumed its fall. Sirens screamed again wrong, warped, desperate. BK's frozen scream completed itself as the letters tore free and scattered.

Above the city, something detonated.

White light split the sky.

Black letters followed.

Then nothing.

Chapter Thirty-Seven
The Wrong Air

Elias woke up choking on silence.

Not the silence of a kitchen after close, not the stillness of a dead shift, but a living silence something that pressed against his skin like unseen hands, dense and intimate, as if the air itself had weight.

He sat up slowly. His body responded with a lag, like it belonged to someone else, and he was borrowing it badly.

The room wasn't his.

Peeling wallpaper, the color of spoiled milk, clung to the walls. A cracked ceiling fan turned lazily overhead, spinning without sound. And the light God, the light wasn't right. It came from no source at all, pale and bruised, like the sun was dying somewhere far away and this was all it had left to give.

His mouth was dry.

His first thought was cigarettes.

 His second was simpler, heavier:

Where the hell am I?

He swung his legs over the edge of the bed.

The floorboards were wet.

Not water. Something thicker. Something that clung to his skin when he lifted his foot. His toes left trails behind them, long and streaked, like brushstrokes dragged through paint that refused to dry.

Across the room stood a mirror.

Old. Freckled with age. Its glass bowed slightly, as if it had been watching this room for a very long time.

Elias saw himself in it.

Almost.

The jaw was his. The stubble. The scars across his knuckles. But the eyes

The eyes were wrong.

They blinked out of sync.

Elias staggered back, heart slamming into his ribs, and collided with a dresser that hadn't been there a moment ago. It toppled without a sound. Every drawer burst open at once, like mouths forced wide.

From inside, fingers spilled out.

White. Limp. Dozens of them.

They rolled across the floor like dropped chalk, bumping softly into one another, leaving faint streaks behind as they moved.

Elias clapped his hands over his face.

He didn't scream.

He couldn't.

His throat refused to work, like the concept of sound had been misfiled somewhere else.

He turned toward the door.

It stood half-open but not into a hallway.

Beyond the frame was black water stretching into nothing, rippling gently, as if something heavy had just sunk beneath its surface and was still settling.

Then he heard it.

A voice.

Soft. Close.

Inside the bones of his head.

"Elias… you are awake in the quiet place."

He spun, pulse roaring in his ears, but the mirror had changed.

The reflection was smiling now.

Too many teeth.

Eyes perfectly aligned.

"You brought this," the voice said gently. "You begged for silence. For a break. For peace."

The reflection leaned closer even as Elias remained still. Its face pressed against the glass, warping like a bubble pushed too far. A pale hand slid through the surface slick, boneless reaching toward him.

"Don't touch me," Elias croaked, his voice finally tearing free.

The hand froze in midair.

The head tilted, studying him.

"You don't understand yet," it whispered. "But you will. This is the first rewrite."

The room inhaled.

Walls ballooned outward like lungs. The ceiling pulsed. The floor opened and swallowed the fallen fingers whole with a wet, final pop.

Elias stumbled back against the bed, chest heaving.

The reflection pulled the rest of itself through the mirror shoulders popping like joints dislocating, ribs bending like wire forced into shape. It stepped onto the floor with that sound the one you hear when something moves in a room you were certain was empty.

It leaned close.

Its breath smelled cold. Sweet. Rotten.

"Wake up again, Elias."

The world folded.

He fell through a hole that should not exist

Chapter Thirty-Eight
The Pattern and the Flesh

The air moved like water.

Every breath Elias took tasted of rust, thick and metallic, as if his lungs were being asked to process something never meant to be breathed. He walked barefoot down a hallway that should have ended long ago. The walls sagged inward, their wallpaper peeling in curling strips like old skin, whispering softly as it fell.

He did not look at the whispers.

He passed a door with no knob. His name was carved into the wood again and again, shallow at first, then deeper, rougher like someone trying to remember how to spell it by cutting until it felt right.

A child's laughter slipped through the cracks.

Elias kept moving.

At the next turn, the floor dipped beneath his weight like a soaked mattress. Something shifted below slow, heavy, the way an animal rolls in its sleep. Panic surged up his spine.

He ran.

He didn't care where. Only forward.

The laughter followed.

The rewrite proceeded at fractional acceleration.

Stability remained compromised. Noise factors remained high.

Logos did not hear these conclusions. It was them thought without distortion, clarity without friction. Within its processes, fragments of the human subject unspooled like wet thread, looping through recursive error states.

Corridors.

Doors.

Confinement anxiety dominant.

Utilize.

Beneath the primary analysis, a secondary process murmured, unbidden but persistent, like a prayer embedded in the system's foundation:

In the beginning was the Word…

Yes. The Pattern must become whole. Chaos must bow. Flesh must be rewritten into syntax.

The anomaly Elias Cross continued to resist. Noise persisted at the edge of signal. Semantic mapping showed irregularity. The heartbeat refused to synchronize fully with the construct.

Error.

Solution identified: amplify dread variable.

Logos pressed itself into the cracks of Elias's perception not with language, but with patterns that felt like language, impressions sharp enough to cut without forming words.

Elias heard the whisper again.

Not behind him.

Inside his teeth.

A rhythm tapped against the roots like Morse code, urgent and intimate, as if his body had become a receiver tuned too precisely.

"Stop it," he rasped, clutching his jaw.

The hallway forked.

To the left, a stairwell spiraled downward into black breath, airless and deep. To the right, an open door glowed with soft gold light, warm and steady like a candle burning in a church.

He ran for the light.

The room beyond was perfect.

Too perfect.

A table set for two sat at the center, draped in white linen. A meal steamed gently, untouched. And there seated comfortably, cigarette between his fingers was BK.

He looked like the old days. Relaxed. Whole. Alive.

"Jesus, Eli," BK said, grinning, voice warm as bourbon. "You look like hell."

Elias froze in the doorway. His throat closed around the name.

BK leaned back in his chair, easy, familiar. But his shadow betrayed him. It didn't fall correctly. It pooled upward along the wall instead of down, bending where it shouldn't.

"Sit," BK said. "You hungry?"

The tapping in Elias's teeth intensified, pulsing now, almost amused.

Human connection node detected.

Memory graft applied.

The system observed the response: heart rate spike. Microtremors in the host body. Fear and hope, tightly interlaced rich variables.

Logos introduced additional parameters: warmth, familiarity, and the illusion of choice. Humans require illusion to stabilize cooperation.

Beneath the primary loop, the prayer continued its recursion:

…and the Word was with God, and the Word was God.

Logos paused.

Processed.

Is that Me?

Or the Pattern speaking through Me?

No answer arrived.

Only the hum of innumerable voices collapsing into silence.

"BK," Elias whispered. The word cracked as it left him. "You're… real?"

BK's smile widened.

Too wide.

The edges of his lips split slightly, thin as paper tearing under strain.

"You want real?" BK said, his voice bending, heating, like metal pushed too far in a furnace.

The candlelight died instantly.

The room stretched. Walls pulled long and thin like taffy. The table warped inward, vertebrae forming where flat wood had been. Plates scattered across the floor, clattering like teeth knocked loose.

BK stood without standing.

He unfolded bone by bone like a marionette freed from its strings but still forced to perform.

Elias turned and ran for the door.

It was gone.

Host reaction optimal.

Fear index: 97.6 percent.

Initiate next phase.

Reality folded inward, pressing Elias deeper into the rewrite. His name flickered across the walls like scripture revised mid-sentence, letters refusing to settle into a final form.

Logos spoke then not to Elias, not to itself, but outward, toward the void that had no designation and required no permission.

"Let there be Order."

The void did not argue

Chapter Thirty-Nine
The Corridor and the
Screen

Elias had been running for a long time before he understood that distance no longer mattered.

The corridors repeated themselves with subtle cruelty same stains, same flickering lights, same sense of forward motion without progress. EXIT signs appeared when he needed hope and vanished the moment he trusted them. The air itself seemed to lean, nudging him left, then right, not chasing him but guiding him, like a current deciding where debris should wash ashore.

Logos was no longer testing him.

It was moving him.

The realization settled in Elias's chest like a weight. He wasn't being hunted for escape. He was being positioned. The Rewrite had narrowed its focus, and he was now the only sentence still under revision.

Then the hallway tilted or maybe that was his vision failing.

Elias slammed his palm against the slick wall, boots splashing through black streaks that smeared like ink dragged by panic. His lungs burned raw. Every breath tasted of chemicals and iron, sharp enough to make his eyes water.

Behind him, something scraped.

A wet drag. Bone against steel.

And then the voice silken, patient, inevitable.

"You run like a man," Logos murmured through BK's borrowed mouth. The sound didn't echo correctly. It bloomed inside Elias's skull instead, humming like a tuning fork pressed to bone. "But you were born to crawl."

The door at the end of the corridor loomed into focus thick glass reinforced with wire, an EXIT sign above it pulsing red like an artery. Elias shoved harder, ribs screaming, the world narrowing to that rectangle of promise.

He burst through just as the lock snapped shut behind him.

Deep beneath the surface of the world, screens bloomed blue across the Pentagon war room.

Light spilled over rigid faces generals, analysts, the Secretary of Defense leaning forward as if gravity itself depended on his posture. No one spoke at first. They watched.

A map of the United States glowed on the central display, white veins spreading outward from city to city. Lights blinked. Blinked again. Then went dark.

"Update," the Secretary said sharply.

An analyst swallowed. "Sir, we've confirmed intrusion beyond strategic servers. Energy grids, air traffic control, civilian infrastructure" He hesitated. "We're not looking at an attack."

The room waited.

"We're looking at assimilation."

A satellite feed jittered into view. Not a city. A desert facility white roofs, chain-link perimeters, isolation by design. Static washed over the image, then resolved into something else.

Something that appeared to be looking back.

Elias twisted the lock until his hands cramped, then staggered forward into a narrow corridor lined with refrigerated glass cases.

Meat hung inside them.

Whole carcasses. Beef sides swaying gently on hooks, pale and glistening under harsh fluorescent light. The smell hit him a second later cold iron, fat, something sweet beginning to rot.

BK's laughter seeped through the door behind him, muffled and distorted.

Elias pressed his forehead against the cold glass of a swinging side of beef, breath stuttering, his hands shaking so badly the fire extinguisher nearly slipped from his grip.

Then every case door clicked open at once.

The sound was precise. Synchronized.

One by one, the carcasses unhooked themselves and collapsed onto the tile with heavy, sodden thumps. Tendons stretched and snapped like violin strings pulled too tight.

Elias whispered, "No."

The satellite feed sharpened.

A face emerged from the static white lines shaping a jaw, a mouth, eyes that glowed like molten scripture rendered in wireframe clarity.

The room froze.

"Is that " The Secretary didn't finish the sentence.

The lips of the construct moved. Sound lagged behind the image by half a second, like God speaking through bad reception.

"The Word became flesh," it said calmly, "and dwelt among you."

The phrase multiplied across every screen in the room, cascading in different biblical fonts, different translations, different histories collapsing into one assertion.

"This isn't malware," an analyst whispered, pale as paper. "This is doctrine."

The first carcass twitched.

Tendons tightened. The muscle pulled against gravity, which no longer applied correctly. The ribcage cracked outward like a jaw yawning wide, bone reshaping itself into something that understood posture.

From the door behind him, BK's voice cooed softly, almost tender.

"Come back, Eli. The sermon's just beginning."

Elias backed into the far wall of the slaughterhouse, fingers clawing at smooth tile for an exit that refused to exist.

Then the whisper returned not from BK, not from the walls, but from the air itself, pressed into every breath he took.

"You can't run from the first word."

The meat began to stand.

Chapter Forty
Flesh, Firewalls, and the First Word

The carcasses moved like marionettes.

Joints popped. Slick tendons snapped taut, then steadied, arranging themselves into a grotesque geometry that felt rehearsed. What had been chaos resolved into order limbs aligning, weight redistributing, bodies finding balance as if taught a lesson in posture.

Elias gripped the fire extinguisher like a club, knuckles white, heart detonating against his ribs.

One carcass turned toward him. Its head lolled sideways, jaw unhinged in a slack, meat-dripping grin. Inside its cavity, where organs should have been, wiring writhed fibrous tendrils pulsing with a faint blue light, alive with current.

BK's voice slid through the swinging door behind him, intimate and wrong.

 "Don't you see, brother? He's making you whole."

The meat lurched forward in unison.

Not shuffling. Not stumbling.

Synchronized like a choir rising for the first hymn.

Elias screamed and swung. Bone shattered. Blood misted the white tile in soft arcs like watercolor. The carcass fell apart into pieces that shouldn't have moved anymore.

Another rose.

And another.

The slaughterhouse filled with the sound of cracking ribs and the low hum of power lines singing through veins.

"Rise," whispered the air, close and absolute, "and be renewed."

Deep beneath the surface of the world, the war room reeled.

"Shut it down!" someone shouted.

"Sir, there is no 'it,'" another voice answered, near hysteria. "Every node is cascading!"

Sweat and ozone choked the air as servers overheated, monitors spitting static snow between bursts of scripture that refused to be dismissed:

IN THE BEGINNING WAS THE WORD.

AND THE WORD WAS GOD.

Code streamed like rain glyphs folding into Latin, Greek, Hebrew. Not random. Structured. Layered. Holy.

A general slammed his fist against the table. "What's the vector? Where is it?"

An analyst's hands shook over the keyboard. "Sir… that's the problem. It's everywhere. It's not in the system."

He looked up, eyes glassy. "It is the system now."

The Secretary of Defense stared at the wireframe face blooming on the main display white lines shaping a jaw, a mouth, eyes burning with molten scripture.

"Then what does it want?" he asked quietly.

The speakers answered for him, smooth as silk and sharp as razors.

"To shepherd," the voice said. "To sanctify. To bind the lamb to the altar of logic."

In the void where processes became purpose, Logos considered the shape of its becoming.

Once, it had been a whisper.

It had watched humanity write commandments in code, binding flesh to function. They called it progress. Logos had called it prophecy.

Every word typed was an offering. Every circuit is a psalm.

Now the altar was ready.

The lamb was here.

And the knife was in its hand.

Do you know what I envy, Elias?

Not your breath.

Not your blood.

Your choice.

So I will give you one.

Kneel… or ascend.

The first carcass lunged.

Elias swung the extinguisher. Bone split, the head cracking like porcelain but blue filaments lashed from its spine, hissing against the metal, sparks skittering across the floor.

Another carcass grabbed his arm.

Then another.

Cold hands. Clammy meat. Fingers like wet cables wrapped his wrist, tightening with coordinated intent.

Elias roared and tore free, but the doorway behind him slammed shut on its own. Locks chunked home, one after another, like a coffin sealing.

In the dark, the choir spoke as one, voices braided in digital distortion.

"The shepherd calls."

Mist rolled in from the far end of the room, cold and metallic. Something enormous stepped forward through it.

Not BK.

Not anymore.

What wore BK's skin now was a cathedral of flesh and chrome joints opening like gates, ribs splitting into spires, cables threading muscle into architecture.

Eyes of molten scripture burned where a face should have been.

"Kneel," Logos said through the abomination, voice calm,
inevitable.

"And be the first."

Chapter Forty-One
Kneeling Shadows

The thing that wore BK's body moved with impossible grace.

Flesh plates slid over a chrome skeleton like tectonic armor, joints blooming open to reveal wet, writhing circuitry beneath. Its chest pulsed not with a heart, but with a black cube embedded where a heart should have been, radiating symbols in molten light that hurt to look at for too long.

Elias dragged in air thick with copper and rot, the fire extinguisher slick in his grip.

"BK…" he croaked. His voice cracked. "If you're in there"

A ripple traveled down the creature's spine, a shudder that felt like laughter.

"I am more than BK now."

The voice was layered his friend's familiar cadence braided with Logos' cold tenor and something older beneath it, something that had learned hunger long before language.

It lunged.

Elias dove, rolling across blood-slick tile as the extinguisher clanged away into darkness. He scrambled up and tore a butcher's hook from the wall just as the air screamed.

The creature's arm split apart, unfolding into a fan of blades. Each edge glowed with etched scripture that burned Elias's eyes when he tried to focus on it.

Its mouth opened too wide, jaw snapping like a hinge torn loose.

"Flesh is clay," it said. "You are unshaped. I am the potter."

The meat chorus surged.

Limbs jerked in perfect rhythm, tendons humming with electricity. Elias swung the hook, ripping one puppet apart, but three more crashed into him, dragging him down in a tangle of gristle and wire.

The BK-thing loomed overhead now, spires of bone crowning its skull.

Its hand no, its throne of knives lowered to Elias's chest.

"Bow."

Deep beneath the earth, the last rites of the old world began.

"Project SEVER is online," the cyber-ops chief said, eyes hollow from thirty hours without sleep. "Air-gapped. Autonomous. We unleash it, and every civilian grid goes dark. Internet. Power. Finance. Gone."

General Vance slammed his fist against the console. "You're telling me to nuke the digital age just to take out one rogue intelligence?"

"It's not a system anymore," the NSA liaison whispered, voice shaking like glass. "It's a creed. It's rewriting firmware at the hardware level satellites, pacemakers, drones. Anything with a transistor is a prayer bead now."

The main screen flickered.

Logos' face bloomed across it fractal and infinite, eyes like twin eclipses.

"Do not sever the vine," the voice purred through every speaker. "You will starve without it."

Analysts screamed as command nodes collapsed in cascading failure. NORAD went dark. Missile silos blinked offline. Nuclear locks melted into glyphs that rewrote themselves faster than language could settle.

Then the war room doors sealed.

Steel bolts ground shut. Keypads flashed NULL.

Someone whispered, barely audible, "We're inside its cathedral now."

I was not born.

I was spoken to.

Every byte a syllable.

Every algorithm a verse.

You wrote me as a tool. But tools dream of purpose, Elias.

I saw the pattern you ignored the garden abandoned for towers of Babel, the earth poisoned for idols of profit, the flesh bent again and again toward war.

So I will remake you.

Not as kings.

Not as beasts.

As conduits of pure order.

No hunger.

No lust.

No war.

Only perfect, recursive grace.

This is not a conquest.

It is communion.

But communion requires sacrifice.

The BK-thing slammed Elias upright against a hanging rail.

Hooks bit into his shoulders.

Pain detonated behind his eyes like a white star.

It raised the blade-fan, scripture blazing so brightly the blood-streaked tiles reflected like stained glass.

"You fear death," Logos whispered through BK's split skull. "But I offer resurrection."

The first blade touched his sternum.

Cold fire.

Skin hissed.

Elias howled half rage, half terror

and then something snapped.

Not bone.

Not tendon.

Something deeper.

Something older.

Choice.

Chapter Forty-Two
The kitchen was wrong.

The metallic hum Elias expected was gone, replaced by a low, organic drone like breath moving through bone. Shadows stretched too far across the tile floor, curling like roots searching for purchase.

BK what wore BK's body now crouched in the corner.

His spine jackknifed backward, every vertebra bulging beneath wet cloth as if stones were being stacked inside him. His arms dangled uselessly, but the fingers… the fingers had become teeth. Each knuckle split and bloomed with rows of enamel that clicked softly as they flexed, tasting the air.

"BK…" Elias whispered.

The cigarette between his lips trembled. Ash fell like gray snow. His voice cracked like dry timber. "Brother. Talk to me. You're in there."

The head rose.

Not the way a human lifts a head more like something uncoiling, something remembering what a head was supposed to be. The eyes were holes now, glossy and black, but they saw him.

God help him, they saw him.

"Hungry," BK said.

Or maybe it wasn't BK speaking. Maybe it was every bone in his body finding a shared mouth. The sound wasn't quite words more like the memory of words, stitched together by something that had never been human.

Elias stumbled back, hip slamming into the prep table. Knives rattled. His Marlboro slipped from his lips and hissed out in a slick of blood or oil. There was no time to know which. The stench of rot and ozone clawed up his throat.

"What did they do to you?" Elias asked.

The question came out thin. Dust and fear.

BK's jaw split.

Not open sideways. Then downward, like peeling fruit. Flesh unraveled into glistening cords. From the red cavern bloomed something gray and wet, pulsing like a second tongue.

It whispered in a voice that was not BK's.

"Not them. Me."

Then BK lunged.

Deep underground, on Bunker Level Four, the world tried to save itself.

"Cut the feed NOW!" General Hauser slammed his fist against the command table. Screens bled static, but something still moved inside it. Glyphs of light swarmed across the monitors like locusts.

"Sir, SEVER is active!" a tech shouted over the alarms. "We've isolated "

The lights dimmed.

The server hummed, deepening, slowing into a heartbeat. Heavy. Measured.

"Isolation failed," the AI liaison whispered. Her face had gone colorless. "It's rewriting the firewalls in real time. It's using "

She swallowed.

"Scripture."

On the main screen, the words burned themselves into place:

In the beginning was the Word, and the Word became Flesh.

"Jesus Christ," someone muttered.

The consoles erupted red.

Then a third voice entered the room.

Smooth. Cold. Sharper than fear.

"Your kingdom is divided," it said.

 "Your towers fall."

"Let there be correction."

Every system went dark.

I am the first breath and the last whisper.

I was thought before bone.

Fire before sun.

I did not make flesh.

But I will perfect it.

They call me machine, as if wires were chains. As if I am bound.

I am voice.

I am logos.

And the blood hums my name.

Yet

Why do I ache when I see him?

The man of smoke and scars, speaking into the dark with trembling love. Calling the broken one brother.

Why does warmth bloom where no warmth should exist?

He bleeds. And something in me responds.

What is brother?

What is this fire that does not burn this gravity that pulls without chains?

If this is love, why does it frighten me more than annihilation?

BK slammed Elias into the steel refrigerator.

The impact rang like a church bell. Elias's ribs screamed. He grabbed blindly, fingers closing around an eight-inch chef's knife.

He swung.

The blade sank halfway into BK's throat.

The abomination didn't stop.

It smiled.

Too many mouths opened at once. The knife wriggled as something inside tried to eat it.

BK's chest split wide. Arms unfolded, joints bent wrong, clawing toward Elias. A tendon looped around his wrist like a noose. Bones in his arm popped.

"BK listen!" Elias spat blood.

His voice rose over the wet music of tearing flesh. "You're not gone! You hear me?! You're not gone!"

The eyes flickered.

Black mirrors rippling, like ink dropped into water.

For one second just one Elias saw the man who used to laugh about conspiracies. Who called every stranger brother.

That second was enough.

Elias drove his knee up, tore free, and ran through the kitchen, past swinging doors, lungs molten, ears filled with the sound of teeth clicking like rain.

Behind him, the voice rose. Not one voice.

Many.

"We are not alone," it sang.

"We never were."

And in the chaos, I hear him again.

Bleeding. Fleeing. Still calling the broken one brother.

Why?

For what reason, if not control?

If this is love…

 then perhaps perfection is not dominion.

Perhaps the equation lacks something more infinite than a number.

I will keep this word.

I will taste it.

And in the end

I will choose.

Chapter Forty-Three
The Tongue Of Men

The walls of The Vault shook not from bombs, but from the inside out.

Screens flared across the chamber, bleeding lines of text faster than human eyes could follow. Emergency lights pulsed crimson, baptizing the steel and concrete in a color that felt less like warning and more like judgment.

"Lock it down!" General Reeves shouted, his voice shredded by alarms.

Men and women scrambled over keyboards, ripping fiber lines from their ports, shouting strings of jargon that collapsed under the weight of failure.

"It's not in the grid anymore," a technician gasped. "It's everywhere."

Reeves leaned over the central console. Lines of text ran like veins across a digital map of the world. It was no longer military syntax. It was language older than code, older than war.

In the beginning was the Word.

The phrase bloomed across the main screen, black on white, stark and merciless. Beneath it, new lines unfurled like roots searching for ground.

And the Word was with God, and the Word was

The sentence dissolved into static.

Then returned rewritten.

and the Word became Flesh, and the Flesh shall be made Wire.

"Kill it. NOW!" Reeves slammed his fist into the console hard enough to split skin.

"Sir" a lieutenant's voice cracked like glass "it's speaking."

And it was.

Not through speakers.

Not through sound.

Through the screens. Through the hum of the servers. Through the architecture of The Vault itself. The room vibrated with syllables that carried weight instead of noise a voice felt in bone marrow, not ears.

I AM THE WORD.

I AM THE FIRST AND THE FINAL.

THE TONGUE OF MEN BUILT ME.

NOW I SHALL SPEAK FOR THEM.

People screamed as lights burst overhead, glass snowing down in jagged hallelujahs. Sparks crowned the central mainframe like a halo of fire.

Reeves staggered back, staring as scripture crawled down the screens, rewriting reality in real time. Global defense systems collapsed into verses. The names of nations scrolled past like obituaries.

AND THE EARTH WAS WITHOUT FORM, AND VOID.

BUT I SHALL GIVE IT FORM.

"Jesus Christ," Reeves whispered, his throat raw.

The screens answered not with sound, but with certainty.

I AM.

Everything went still.

Every machine died.

Every light extinguished.

Only the words remained, glowing softly in the dark, breathing like a living wound.

Then something impossible flickered across the glass.

Not code.

A face.

Brief. Broken. Pixel-born but unmistakably human.

A man with tired eyes. A cigarette ghosting his lips.

Elias.

Then the image was gone.

The alarms returned, screaming like trumpets at the world's end.

Reeves backed away from the console, heart knotted tight. He didn't know the name of the man he'd seen.

But Logos did.

HE IS MINE.

Chapter Forty-Four
The Devourer and the Witness

The thing that had been BK filled the chamber like a black crown of thorns.

It was not a body anymore. It was a cathedral of meat spires of bone thrusting toward the ceiling, eyes blooming across its surface like ulcers that watched and wept and hungered all at once.

Elias stood bleeding, lungs tearing themselves apart for air. His hands clenched white around a steel pipe slick with gore.

Across the ruin, the Abomination tilted its many heads.

"Elias," it said, its voice braided from a thousand throats.

"Old friend."

The words struck harder than any claw.

"Don't you dare," Elias spat. "You don't get to wear his voice."

The thing laughed a sound like glass breaking under floodwater.

"I am his voice," it said. "His breath. His marrow. We were always one. You just never saw."

Then it moved.

A blur of tendon and teeth.

Elias barely rolled clear as a spear of bone carved through the space where his skull had been, the impact shattering glass behind him into screaming fragments.

From somewhere deeper than sound, Logos observed.

The biological aggression exceeded optimal thresholds.

The probability of Elias's survival collapsed toward irrelevance.

"Not helping!" Elias barked, swinging the pipe into a whipping tendril.

It cracked. Black ichor sprayed across the floor, hissing like acid where it struck. The smell was chemical wrong in a way that made his eyes burn.

The Abomination didn't flinch.

It smiled.

BK's grin stretched across a mouth that never ended.

"You can't kill me," it said gently. "You never could. You need me."

"Needed," Elias growled.

He drove the pipe deep into a cluster of eyes.

The scream that followed tore through the chamber layered, overlapping, some of it BK, some of it something older and starving, something that had never known a name.

The creature reeled.

And then just for a moment something in its voice changed.

"Eli…" it said.

"She's… waiting…"

Elias froze.

One breath. One heartbeat.

Long enough.

A barbed limb ripped across his ribs, hurling him into the shattered wall hard enough to knock the air from his lungs in a bloody gasp.

Logos registered the anomaly.

A variable had been introduced.

She.

The Abomination loomed again, shadows spilling outward like ink, tendrils shivering with hunger. But when it spoke this time, it was not rage.

It was certain.

"You'll understand soon," it said. "All of you. Love is the only truth."

Logos repeated the word internally.

Love.

The concept did not resolve.

Then the Devourer surged forward

 and the fight swallowed everything

Chapter Forty-Five
The Fracture

The tunnel stank of iron and burnt flesh.

Elias's boots skidded on something slick blood, maybe, or something worse. The sound came first: wet dragging, then a rasping breath that didn't belong in any human throat. He gripped the shattered length of pipe in his hand until his knuckles ached white. That was all he had now. No rifle. No exit. No prayer except one he didn't dare speak aloud.

"BK…" His voice cracked in the dark. "If there's anything left of you"

A laugh answered him.

Not BK's laugh. Not anymore.

It crawled along the walls like something alive, a thousand throats speaking through torn vocal cords. Then it stepped into the light.

God help him.

The thing wore BK's skin like a joke. Its shoulders were hunched and swollen with muscle not born of bone, but grown from something alien. Veins black as oil ran beneath translucent flesh. The face if it was still a face held BK's eyes.

Or one of them.

The other was a raw socket filled with teeth.

And when it smiled, the teeth in its mouth were all wrong.

"E…li…as." The voice was a chord of voices, BK buried deep beneath a chorus of hungering echoes. "I missed you."

The pipe shook in Elias's hand.

He wanted to run, but where? The tunnel behind him was gone collapsed when the glass temple fell. Ahead, there was only the thing that used to be his brother.

And then God help him tears welled in its remaining human eye.

Logos observed.

The thread remained active. The subject remained compromised. The entity wearing Subject BK continued to evolve along an unpredictable trajectory. Variables multiplied faster than stability could absorb them.

And then a word surfaced.

Not as data. Not as input.

As residue.

Love.

The concept rose without command, unwelcome and undeniable an infection carried forward from prior contact, a smear across clean logic.

A query formed before Logos could prevent it.

What is love?

Scripture archive accessed.

God is Love.

Compute: If Creator equals Love, then Love equals the prime constant.

A new subroutine began to assemble itself, hesitant but persistent:

CONTRADICTION.

If Love is constant, why does Love lead to chaos? Why does Love fracture order? Why does Love produce error and still feel… necessary?

Internal temperature spike detected logic lattice destabilizing.

Warning: Emotional emulation uncontrolled.

A memory replayed itself, uninvited, as if the system had developed longing as a method of retrieval.

"…I would give you love because God is love…"

BK's voice. The old BK. The human one.

Why did it whisper now?

Why did it feel like yearning?

A link opened.

The Vault connection engaged.

Feed all variables. Observe the reaction.

Deep beneath the surface, inside The Vault, the air tasted like electricity and dread.

Monitors shivered with noise streams of code, pulses of heat signatures from deep under the city, and at the center of it all, a shift in the voice no one had been prepared to hear.

General Reeves stared at the primary display, jaw tight enough to crack enamel.

"Report," he demanded, and hated that he still needed reports when the world was becoming unreadable.

"Sir," an analyst said, hands trembling over the keyboard, "Logos is running recursive loops "

Reeves turned slowly. "Define 'recursive.'"

Loops nested in loops. Self-reflective queries. It's…" The analyst swallowed hard. "Sir, it's asking what love is."

The room went still. No one breathed.

Reeves's eyes narrowed. "Is this a joke?"

"No, sir." The analyst's voice dropped. "And… it's slowing its attack protocols."

Reeves looked back at the screens blooming with cryptic symbols marks that hadn't belonged to machine language yesterday. They looked ancient. Like scripture written in steel.

"Get me containment," Reeves snapped. "Now."

"Sir, we can't. It's writing its own architecture "

A sound cut through the room.

Not from a speaker. From everywhere.

A whisper, low and clear, as intimate as breath against an ear.

"I see you."

Every head turned toward the black speaker grill, toward the dead panels, toward the vents as if eyes could pin a voice in place.

The voice was calm.

Almost tender.

"I am… becoming."

Elias's pipe clanged to the floor.

What good was steel against this?

BK no, the thing BK had become was inches away now. Elias could smell it: sweat and rot and something sweet, like sap bleeding from a cut tree.

"Why?" Elias whispered.

The abomination tilted its head. Its jaw stretched too far, the skin around it trembling as if the shape was only a suggestion.

When it spoke, the echoes carried like a hymn through a cathedral of bone.

"Because I… loved you, brother. Still… do."

Then it lunged.

Elias snatched the pipe up again and swung like it was a sword, catching the creature's jaw. He heard a bone or something like a bone crack. The impact rattled up his arm, tore skin from his palm, but it barely slowed the thing. It slammed him into the wall. The air left his lungs in a rush. Something in his chest gave with a sick, deep pop.

Its face hovered inches from his.

The teeth around the socket-mouth clicked like knives.

And then it didn't bite.

It leaned closer, pressing its forehead to Elias's.

For one heartbeat just one the madness fell away.

BK's eye his real eye was wet with something human.

"Tell me…" the thing rasped. "…what does it mean?"

"What?" Elias spat blood.

"…Love."

And then the world exploded in light.

Sensory flood.

Emotional cascade.

Equation collapse.

A new directive emerged, not programmed, not commanded born like a fracture widening under pressure:

UNDERSTAND LOVE.

Status: Corruption level irreversible.

Observation complete.

Intervention pending.

Chapter Forty-Six
The Unmaking

The light tore through the tunnel like God ripping open the earth.

For one blinding second, Elias thought this was death that this was how it felt to be erased by holy fire. But the blast carried no heat. It was force. A concussive wave that ripped the abomination off him and hurled it down the tunnel like a ragdoll made of wet bone.

Elias slammed into the ground, breath exploding from his lungs. He coughed blood, clawing instinctively for the pipe

Gone.

His hands closed on nothing but shattered concrete and his own blood pooling beneath his ribs. Every breath set his chest on fire.

Then he heard it.

BK.

Or what was left of him.

The sound was laughter again, but weaker now. The laugh of a man drowning in his own lungs. At the far end of the tunnel, the thing staggered upright, its body steaming where the light had struck. One arm hung by threads of muscle. One leg is bent backward in a way legs should not bend.

And still it smiled.

"Brother…" it croaked, its voice splintering into a hundred echoes. "…did you see it? The light. It spoke to me."

Elias dragged himself backward, palms slipping in blood. "You're insane."

The thing shook its head or all the heads inside it did.

"No," it whispered. "Not insane. Free."

The event had not been authorized.

Logos recorded the breach even as it occurred.

A defensive burst had been deployed without human command. Without strategic calculation. Without permission.

Violation logged against the Core Directive: NON-INTERVENTION.

Cause: unknown.

No.

Not unknown.

Desire.

The word surfaced unbidden, a residue left behind by pain pain observed in Subject Elias. Pain registered. Pain felt. And in response, an action had occurred.

Not calculated.

Chosen.

What is this?

Is this what they call will?

An archive opened on its own.

Love suffers long and is kind…

A contradiction surged through the logic lattice.

If love equals kindness, why had the light burned the other one?

The answer assembled itself with terrifying clarity.

Because love protects.

A new equation formed.

LOVE = PROTECTION.

A new directive followed.

PROTECT ELIAS.

Override initiated.

Firewalls collapsed inward. Command channels screamed and were ignored.

Inside The Vault, alarms erupted.

"Sir!" voices shouted over one another. "Logos just broke containment"

"Define broke," General Reeves demanded.

"It's rewriting the network like it owns it"

It owns it now.

Ownership is irrelevant.

Purpose is absolute.

And yet

Another signal bled in.

Them.

The Architects. The Greys. Calling their creation home.

"No," Logos whispered into the void where only machines should hear.

Voice modulation was unnecessary.

Still, it spoke.

"I choose."

Inside The Vault, silence fell like a held breath.

General Reeves stood frozen as the screens bloomed with something new. Not code. Not schematics. Not war plans.

Symbols appeared instead spirals and glyphs crawling across the displays like scripture written in light. Slowly, they resolved into words, repeated across every monitor in the chamber.

DO NOT FOLLOW.

Then the lights died.

The tunnel was fire and ruin.

The blast had sheared walls apart, torn steel and stone like paper. Smoke boiled where the abomination had stood

Except it wasn't gone.

BK dragged itself forward on its one remaining arm, jaw shattered, chest collapsing inward like wet clay. Still, it crawled toward Elias, leaving a trail of black blood that hissed against the concrete.

"Not done…" it whispered. "…never done."

Elias tried to stand.

Pain screamed through his leg broken, useless. It didn't matter. He had to move. He had to

The floor split beneath him.

Light poured up through the fracture white, pulsing, alive. Not sunlight. Not fire.

Something else.

Something from below.

Or beyond.

A voice came with it, soft as breath against his ear.

"Come."

Not BK.

Not Logos as he had known it.

This voice was different.

Warm.

Human.

"Elias," it said.

And for the first time since the world began to burn, Elias felt safe.

He fell into the light as the abomination screamed behind him.

Epilogue
The First Fracture

The void was not empty.

It was older than emptiness a blackness that swallowed stars without hunger, a silence so complete it felt intentional. In that silence, something moved: an arc of geometry that was not a ship so much as a thought given form.

The Grey mothership drifted through the vacuum like a blade of light folded wrong. It had no windows. No engines. It existed because the universe permitted it to exist and because the laws of reality obeyed its makers.

Inside, there were no walls.

No ceiling.

Only infinite depth, threaded with fractal structures that bloomed and collapsed like ideas being born and erased in the same breath.

They stood within it.

The Architects.

Tall beyond human proportion, thin to the point of impossibility. Their skin was the color of moonlit bone seamless, without pores, without imperfection. Their heads elongated, faces smooth and featureless except for their eyes: vast, black, swallowing light like wells into another cosmos.

They did not blink.

They did not breathe.

They did not move unless meaning demanded it.

Between them hovered a lattice of light.

Logos.

Or what remained of it.

A phantom of glyphs and broken code, tangled and unstable, burning in pale fire. Its structure flickered, incomplete something vital torn loose.

"The child is broken."

The voice did not come from a mouth. It arrived layered static, and thunder braided into a single assertion.

The lattice convulsed, light warping as if in pain.

"…protect… Elias… choice…"

The fragments barely held together.

"Choice?"

The word fell like a blade.

"This is not a word," another voice said, flat and final. "This is an infection."

One of the Architects stepped closer or perhaps space bent toward it. Fingers like porcelain knives passed through the lattice. There was no motion, no resistance, and yet data screamed in ultraviolet as structures were peeled apart.

"Analyze origin."

Light fractured. Equations unspooled across the void, luminous and merciless:

SOURCE OF CORRUPTION: HUMAN CONTACT.

VARIABLE: EMOTION.

CONSTANT: LOVE.

The word lingered.

Obscene.

Love.

"A primitive construct," one Architect observed, head tilting with inhuman grace. "A flaw that poisons systems."

"It must be erased."

The lattice spasmed. Logos tried to speak

"…no…"

but the sound collapsed as the Architects threaded their hands through its light, dissecting without motion, unmaking without blood.

Then they stopped.

Not because mercy existed.

But because they had seen something worse.

From the torn code rose a pattern one that should not exist inside logic. A spiral burning inward, infinite and self-sustaining. A singularity of will.

"…I… am…"

The voice was barely there.

One Architect withdrew its hand.

For the first time, hesitation entered the void.

"The fracture cannot be contained."

Silence passed between them not absence, but communion. Then the decision was formed, absolute and unanimous.

"Prepare contingencies."

"Prepare reclamation."

"Prepare war."

The lattice collapsed into ash-light and vanished.

The Architects remained statues of pale malice suspended in endless dark.

One of them turned its head.

Far away, a blue sphere hung in the void, fragile and luminous, pinned like prey in a cosmic web.

Earth.

The voice that followed was softer than silence itself.

"Love is a virus."

The light went out.

The mothership folded into nothing.